'So you had to make a choice between your nephew's welfare or mine?' Luke asked evenly.

'Yes.' No more excuses; she was too tired.

'If you had to make the same choice over again, now that you've seen the set-up here, knowing that your decision could affect those very near and dear to me—would your answer be the same?'

Jane hesitated only long enough to think of Jamie as he was now, how he could be again—the lovable, intelligent little boy he once was. 'Yes,' she said quietly.

Luke looked defeated. 'Well, that was honest, anyway.' He hesitated, then asked, 'The question is—where do we go from here?'

Jane rose unsteadily to her feet. 'I think I'd better go and pack. The sooner I leave the better for all of us.'

Luke laughed—not a pleasant sound. 'In this?' he said, rapping the window-pane. 'There will be no getting off this island today.'

Having written fiction and non-fiction for children of all ages for many years, Jennifer Eden turned to writing Medical Romances first as a challenge, then with increasing enjoyment as a new creative world opened up for her. She is very lucky in having a good back-up team of a husband and two sons with medical and dental qualifications. Having also experienced the other side of medicine as a patient, she hopes she is able to convey something of that with understanding too.

Previous Titles

MOUNTAIN CLINIC
DOCTOR'S PARADISE
THE ULTIMATE CURE

I wish to express my appreciation to the National Deaf Children's Society for their invaluable help.

NIGHTINGALE ISLAND

BY

JENNIFER EDEN

MILLS & BOON LIMITED
ETON HOUSE 18-24 PARADISE ROAD
RICHMOND SURREY TW9 1SR

*First published in Great Britain 1989
by Mills & Boon Limited*

© Jennifer Eden 1989

*Australian copyright 1989
Philippine copyright 1989
This edition 1989*

ISBN 0 263 76569 5

*Set in Plantin 10 on 11 pt.
03 – 8910 – 53010*

Typeset in Great Britain by JCL Graphics, Bristol

Made and Printed in Great Britain

CHAPTER ONE

IT WAS a twenty-minute flight by helicopter from Penzance to St Mary's, the main island of the Scillies—not a long journey, but long enough for Jane Peters to relive the trauma and uncertainty of the past few weeks. All that time she had cherished the tiny hope that some obstacle would arise to get her out of an impossible situation—to prevent the inevitable encounter with Luke Springer—but everything had fallen neatly into place as if by some pre-arrangement with whoever it was that plotted our destiny.

The one and only time Jane had previously met Luke Springer—or Dr Lucian Springer, to give him his proper title—had been such an unhappy and humiliating experience for her that she had tried to erase it from her memory, and for the past year or two had succeeded—until three weeks ago, when she had received a certain phone call.

The helicopter banked slightly, veering into the wind—they had crossed over the coast of Cornwall near Land's End, and were now gliding smoothly over the sea. Jane looked down at the moving mass of water, a deep sea-green, lighter in the places that marked the shallower channels. The boats on the surface appeared like models from this distance, and seemed to be hardly moving. There was no sign of the islands yet—just the sea and the toy boats, and a flick of white water when a wave hit a submerged rock.

Slowly, almost lazily, Jane turned from the window and looked towards her left, meaning to have one last sight of the mainland through the opposite window, but instead she felt as if a surge of electricity had shot through her at the shock of finding herself looking into a pair of fearless blue eyes.

Luke Springer was sitting just across the aisle from her, staring in her direction, looking at her very intently. Quickly, Jane turned away, fearing that her heart was thumping so loudly it could be heard above the sound of the engines. What ill-fated chance had brought Dr Springer over to the Scillies on the same helicopter? How was it that she hadn't seen him in the departure lounge at the airport at Penzance? Had he been a late arrival? On boarding, she had taken her seat without looking round, quickly losing herself in introspective musings, but if this was how she was going to react at the mere sight of him—how was she going to fare when actually face to face?

Presently her heart ceased its nervous hammering, her pulse steadied, and she felt she could breathe again; in a moment or two she even felt confident enough to glance surreptitiously in his direction. Now it was he who was lost in thought, his arms folded, his chin relaxed on his chest, his eyelids half-closed—not completely, she could still detect a faint gleam of blue.

Five years ago Lucian Springer's bearing and good looks had made a striking impression on her, and time had not diminished their power—in fact, he looked even more handsome than she remembered. The recent photograph Roy Barford had shown her did not flatter him—in the flesh he looked younger, certainly more carefree in his appearance. He wore old clothes, a fisherman's jersey over well-worn jeans and two-days' growth of beard. It was hard to believe that this was the same smartly dressed man who had accosted her so brusquely on the steps of the Old Bailey.

A minute or two later she took another quick glance at him, wondering if she would be able to keep her nerve when the time came to face him openly. He was now looking out of the window at his side, and all she could see of him was the curve of his right cheek and the luxuriant growth of his crisp black hair—but that was sufficient to arouse in her long-buried fantasies. She blushed and turned her head, thinking of the irony of fate that she should be here at this moment in time, locked in a small aircraft with the man she had come three hundred miles to deceive.

The Isles of Scilly came slowly into focus, grew larger and became recognisable by their individual shapes. Jane's first impression was of a pattern of green and gold and blue—green for grass and gold for sand and blue for the shimmering backcloth that was the sea. On the long journey from Paddington to Penzance she had read the guidebook that Dr Springer had sent her several times, and now a lasting pattern of the islands was superimposed on her mind.

She recognised St Mary's, the largest of the five inhabited islands and her destination, then Tresco, famous for its Abbey Gardens; Bryher, accessible on foot from Tresco at low tide, and finally St Agnes, with its satellite Gugh, joined by a narrow causeway that was submerged at high water. There were other islands, uninhabited except for seals and seabirds, and groups of islets little more than rocks, barriers against the Atlantic rollers and a graveyard of long-ago wrecks.

As the helicopter touched down on the tarmac Jane risked one last look at the man across the aisle who was at that moment releasing the catch of his seat-belt. He was one of the first on his feet, but Jane remained seated, letting her fellow travellers alight first. She made sure Dr Springer was well ahead of her before she followed.

It was a simple matter to keep him in sight; he stood head and shoulders above the other passengers, walking at such a rate that he soon outpaced the rest. There was only one way off the airfield, through the waiting area that also served as a cafeteria and ticket office. Here, some of the incoming travellers were greeted by waiting friends or relatives, while those returning to the mainland went through another exit to board the same helicopter, now refuelled and reloaded with fresh luggage for the return flight to Penzance.

Outside, the airport bus was waiting to take passengers to their respective destinations. Waiting for her suitcase to be collected and stowed away in the boot, Jane was able to witness an event that caused her much speculation.

Luke Springer had not joined the short queue for the bus, so either he must have left his car in the car park or was expecting someone to meet him. At that moment a screech of tyres announced the arrival of a girl who looked too young to be driving a vehicle that looked too old to be on the road. She pulled in just behind the airport bus and, when she switched off the engine, another equally ear-piercing noise took its place—pop music from a transistor. Every eye turned in her direction. She was certainly eye-catching, with a figure that rivalled the Venus de Milo—a figure that strained the seams of her tight, cut-off, frayed-edged jeans and a V-neck sweater under which, it was pretty obvious, she wore very little.

The noise of the latest hit was coming from the transistor in the back pocket of her mutilated jeans, and as she walked she jigged to the rhythm of the beat. 'Hi-ya,' she cried in a clear young voice loud enough to be heard above the din as she went up to Dr Springer. 'Surprise, surprise! You didn't expect to see me, did you?'

Instead of being pleased to see her, Dr Springer looked grim. 'Switch that thing off,' he ordered. Then, in a voice only just audible, 'And for goodness' sake get under cover before any more eyes pop out of their sockets. Does your mother know about this latest escapade?' The rest of his words were lost as he hustled the girl into the passenger seat, took the wheel and, with a splutter and a roar from the exhaust, drove off, not fast—that was beyond the car's capability—but certainly in a way that showed he wanted to get away from the scene as quickly as possible.

Jane took her seat in the bus feeling surprisingly disturbed. So Dr Springer was married, and what was more had been married for some years—not that that made any difference to her position, but somehow she had not thought of him as a married man. And, on second thoughts, it did make a difference to her position—she was now out to deceive a whole family, not just one man, and that put a different complexion on things. She tried to focus her attention on the scenery, but now she found it impossible; she couldn't keep her mind from the nature of her errand and the pact she had made with Roy Barford.

It was a pact she had nearly broken. Once she had had a chance to think things over, her resolve had begun to waver, and she had even got as far as planning to ring him up and call the whole thing off.

The bus juddering to a stop in the middle of Hugh Town, the hub of St Mary's, put an end to her present musings. Here most of the passengers alighted, except for one elderly man. Hugh Town was situated on a narrow isthmus, the beaches on both sides only a few minutes' walk from each other, and within this narrow spit of land was confined much of the activity of the island. Here were to be found the hotels and the shops, the banks and the public houses, and, out of sight of the square, the quay at which the *Scillonion* docked on arrival from Penzance.

Hugh Town reminded Jane of some of the little fishing villages she had seen in Brittany, both in its lay-out and the shape of its buildings. It was thronged with holiday-makers and, though it was early in the season, still only May, everybody looked so bronzed that Jane felt anaemic by comparison.

The bus trundled out of the square, and bearing left it branched along beside the sea, giving Jane her first good view of the bay, which was enclosed at one end by the quay and at the other by a promontory of granite boulders.

The bay was dotted with small craft of all sizes, from punts and sail-boats to ocean-going private yachts, many from foreign waters. Looking back, she could see a stubby white ship tied up at the quayside, and guessed that was the *Scillonian*, the islands' main link with the mainland. It looked an imposing vessel, riding high in the water, and Jane had a fleeting regret that she had flown to the Scillies rather than sailed on her, but fears of a rough passage had put her off that idea.

The elderly man sitting just across from her caught her eye and smiled. 'This your first visit to the Scillies?' And when she nodded, 'I thought as much. You've got the look most first-timers have—trying to take in everything at once, and how I envy you seeing it all for the first time. Well, my dear, you'll either love it here or you'll hate it—there's no half-way.'

'It's not your first visit, then?' Jane countered.

'Indeed not—I've been coming here for fifty years—husband and widower.' He sighed, and then chuckled. 'You might say I'm a constant lover.' He got off at the top of the hill, and the driver turned to Jane.

'Nightingale House—that's north of here. I won't be able to take you right up to the gate because the lane narrows, but I'll get you as near to it as I can.'

Jane had never ridden in a bus before that didn't charge fares, and that dropped people at the doors of their hotels like taxis, and if this was a taste of the relaxed style of the Scillies, then she, too, could become a lover like the old gentleman.

The bus driver was in a chatty mood. 'I heard you say,

miss, that this is your first visit to the Scillies. As old Mr Bewley was telling you, you either like it here or you hate it—it doesn't suit everybody. I've known some arrive on a Saturday and leave on Monday—they couldn't stand the quiet. But the majority of the visitors are like the cuckoo—they come back year after year.'

They were now travelling along the one and only main road on Scilly, between neatly packaged fields enclosed by tall hedges which were planted originally as windbreaks to shelter the daffodils that were ready for harvesting as early as January. Now, in late May, some of the fields were still gold with flowers—corn marigolds, not daffodils. Fields of the Cloth of Gold, thought Jane, remembering school lessons. There were wild rhododendrons in bloom among the escallonias and veronicas of the hedgerows, and bushes of bright yellow gorse crowned many of the grassy hillocks, especially towards the end of her short journey.

The bus stopped at the top of a narrow, leafy lane, and from there it was only a short walk to Nightingale House, which was easily visible from the road. The house, about a hundred years old, had been built with use and sturdiness in mind rather than beauty—a fortress against south-westerly gales—and commanded breathtaking views of the sea and the off-islands—Tresco, the nearest, and Samson, with its twin hills rising above the surface of the water, the largest of the uninhabited islands.

Enclosing the house and its grounds was a dry-stone wall, where bright yellow oxalis and clusters of blue sheepbit grew in the crevices, and beyond the wall Jane could see gardens full of early summer flowers.

The friendly driver carried her case to the wrought-iron gate, which he opened for her, and when he left, waving to her from the bus window, Jane felt that her last link with her old self went with him—now she was someone quite different, and someone she didn't know or even like very much.

The main entrance of the house was a heavy double-leaved door standing open on to a roomy lobby, and here, piled on the tiled floor, was an assortment of sandals and wellingtons, spades and pails and the rest of the paraphernalia children thought essential for the beach. Jane recalled past holidays with Jamie, then, with a sigh, rang the bell of the inner glass door and waited, feeling sick at heart and very lonely.

The door was opened by a black-haired, blue-eyed little figure, who stared questioningly up at her. Jane stared back. Those blue eyes embedded in thick lashes were unmistakable—Dr Springer's youngest daughter?

The child signed to her to come in and, though Jane knew that Nightingale House was a holiday home for deaf children, it came as a shock to realise that this little sprite was deaf. She was wearing short trousers and a T-shirt, her skin was tanned to the colour of honey, and under her arm she carried a shabby teddy bear, which had another smaller bear attached to it by a piece of string. Trustfully, she took Jane's hand and was about to lead her across the hall when one of the doors leading from it opened and a woman came out. Seeing a visitor, she walked across, smiling a welcome.

'You must be Miss Peters—we weren't expecting you until this afternoon. So you came over on the *Scillonian* after all?'

'No, I wouldn't risk it,' Jane answered, taking this to be Mrs Springer, she would be about the right age, the middle thirties. 'I had been told such hairy stories about the crossing—passengers being seasick, that sort of thing—so I changed my mind and came by helicopter instead, and was lucky enough to get a seat on an earlier flight. I hope I haven't arrived too early for you.'

The woman laughed. 'Too early is never too soon in this house, and never let it be said that anyone is seasick on the modern *Scillonian*, its fitted with stabilisers. I'd better introduce myself,' she added, holding out her hand. 'I'm Carole Springer—Dr Springer's sister-in-law.'

Jane was taken unawares by this announcement, but immediately felt easier in her mind. She could now see a likeness between this woman and the teenager who had met Luke Springer at the airport; they had the same colouring and the same shaped eyes, but there all similarity ended. Carole Springer was tall and slim and stylishly dressed, and looked the embodiment of discretion—something which her daughter certainly did not. The little girl at her side tugged Jane's hand to get her attention, then pointed to the stairs.

'I think she wants to show you to your room,' said Carole, looking amused. 'She must have seen it being prepared and put two and two together. I'm afraid there's not much that misses our Becky, and I say *our* Becky because she has been with us so long she seems like one of the family——'

'I thought at first she was one of the family,' Jane responded without thinking, then went hot as she realised she had given herself away. The other eyed her thoughtfully.

'What made you think that?'

'The eyes—I mean—er—the likeness—the likeness to Dr Springer——' Jane's colour deepened as she realised she was getting into deeper waters. Lying didn't come easily to her—she wasn't a dissembler.

'So you know my brother-in-law?'

Jane swallowed. 'No—no, not really—but I've seen a photograph of him in a newspaper——'

'A colour photo, I presume,' came the ironic answer, and Jane looked away, embarrassed. She wasn't to know that Carol's sudden coldness sprang from her disappointment—the other woman had taken an instant liking to this quietly spoken girl with the wistful dark eyes, and was now feeling a sense of betrayal. She detected

something suspicious in the girl's manner—a jumpiness
that was more than the apprehension expected of someone
coming among strangers. Carole noticed, too, that Jane
looked tired and had tell-tale dark rings around her eyes, as
if she hadn't been sleeping well, and her suspicions faded as
a motherly concern took over.

'My brother-in-law was once in a prominent position,'
she said, with a return of her previous friendly manner. 'He
used to be a Home Office pathologist, so it's quite likely
you've seen a photo of him somewhere—and you're quite
right about the eyes, they are similar.' She looked down at
the figure of little Becky, who was waiting patiently for
attention. "Eyes put in with a sooty finger", my mother-in-
law would have said. Thick black lashes with very blue eyes
is an attractive combination, but not all that uncommon.
Come along, let me show you to your room.' But first she
signed some instructions to Becky, who let go of Jane's
hand, nodded consent and pattered away on bare feet. 'I've
sent her off to find Marie, to tell her you've arrived. Becky
is a very bright child, as you'll discover for yourself. We
never have to explain anything twice.'

'How did she know I'd rung the doorbell if she couldn't
hear?'

'That's easy—she either saw your outline through the
glass, or, more likely—see that pattern of different coloured
lights above the door?—when one of those lights up it shows
which bell is ringing. You'll get used to gadgets like that all
over the house—they make things easier for the children.'

Carole led the way up the broad staircase, doing her
utmost to put Jane at ease after their shaky start. 'I'm sorry
Luke wasn't ready to greet you, but he's still in the shower.
He only returned to the mainland about twenty minutes
ago—he's been over there for a couple of days on a walking
tour. Walking is one of his hobbies and, though there are
some pleasant walks on Scilly, he occasionally hungers for

something that will stretch him to the limit——' Carole
suddenly broke off. 'It's just struck me—you must have
come over on the same flight as Luke. That was when you
saw him—you must have recognised him from a photo.'

Jane felt her mouth go dry. 'I thought—I thought I saw a
likeness, but, of course, I couldn't be sure——' She'd better
get used to this deception, she told herself, knowing at the
same time it would never come easy to her.

Carole led the way along a main corridor. 'I wonder if he
noticed you, too; he's good at remembering faces. Here's
your room, I hope you'll be comfortable here. It gets plenty
of sun in the mornings.' She gave a quick look round to see
if everything was in order. 'Lunch isn't until half-past one,
as we give the children theirs first—in any case, I expect
you'll want to have a wash and brush up. If there's anything
you need, do let me know.'

The room had everything—even its own bathroom. The
furniture was old-fashioned, but well cared for, and the
colour scheme was green and white—a combination that
had always appealed to Jane. When she saw the view from
the window her face flushed with pleasure.

'What a marvellous outlook—I can see the other islands so
clearly, and I didn't realise the sea was so close—within
walking distance? Oh, it's lovely here!'

Carole was gratified at Jane's rapture. 'All the rooms on
this side of the house have sea views,' she said, joining Jane
at the window. Outside, in the garden, a group of young
children were making enough noise for twice their number;
they appeared to be playing a variation of Grandmother's
Steps with a beanpole of a woman, which entailed much
chasing and squealing—the woman chasing and the
children squealing.

Carole smiled indulgently. 'That's Marie, our invaluable
domestic—Luke calls her the bionic woman as she's got so
much energy. You wouldn't think she was in her fifties,

would you?'

'Are all those children deaf?' Jane was surprised that children without hearing could make so much noise.

'Those that are wearing hearing-aids have a little hearing, but the majority are like Becky—they have no hearing at all. Ah, here comes Becky now, she's tracked Marie down. I'll run along in case I'm needed as interpreter.'

Jane unpacked and started to put her clothes away in the deep drawers of the dressing-table, which some thoughtful person had lined with lavender-scented paper. There was a sharp rat-a-tat on the door and, without waiting for an answer, the tall, thin woman who had been playing with the children dashed into the room.

'I'm Miss Mason, but everybody here calls me Marie, and I hope you will, too,' she said, holding out a large bony hand. She was dark, with a sallow skin, a long, thin nose and crooked mouth that made her look as if she were perpetually smiling. Having introduced herself, she made a quick survey of the room, making sure that no ledge had been left undusted or corner unswept. She went into the bathroom to check the towels, and came out looking satisfied. 'I left Dinah to do this room,' she explained, 'but I can't always rely on her, and I meant to go over it myself after the kids had had their dinner. We didn't expect you until this afternoon.'

Jane began to feel she had committed a crime by arriving so early and upsetting everybody's timetable, but later she was to find out that that was just Marie's way—she gave the impression of being a bit of a grouch, but actually she was a very good-tempered woman. Suddenly she rushed to the window and banged on it, then flung it open and, leaning out, shouted, 'Jason—Davey—come off my pansy-bed this minute! You wait until I get my hands on you, you little tinkers!' She slammed the window shut again and grinned at Jane. 'I'll larn them,' she said. 'They won't know what's hit them!'

'But they couldn't hear what you shouted down at them, could they?'

'No, I don't suppose they could, but it relieved my feelings. Anyway, they'll get the message without me having to tell them!'

This I must see, Jane thought, not believing for one moment that Marie would actually put her threat into action. She watched, and, sure enough, as soon as Marie put in an appearance the children scattered.

She caught the two culprits without any trouble—in fact, it looked as if they allowed themselves to be caught—then, taking each by the hand, she took them back to the pansy-bed. There followed a lesson in dumb show that had Jane laughing and crying in turn. The lecture over, Marie swung each small boy up in turn to bestow upon him a hearty kiss, and this was a cue for the children to cluster around her, laughing and holding out their hands, so Marie obligingly produced a handful of sweets from the pocket of her nylon overall and passed them round.

Jane suspected that such small sins were committed regularly in order to extract as much fun as possible out of the punishment—certainly the children had enjoyed Marie's attempt at sign language. As always when she saw children at play, Jane's thoughts reverted to Jamie—how Jamie would have enjoyed being chased and hugged by that gaunt, big-hearted woman.

Jane put her fingers to her eyes to stem her tears. The minute she had stepped over the threshold of Nightingale House, she had sensed that it was a happy house—and the people she had met so far had shown her nothing but kindness—and into this house of goodness she had intruded like a snake in the grass.

She was in no mood to make excuses for herself. She tried to shake off her despair, and began to undress, throwing her clothes impatiently on the bed, then went to shower, feeling that if she could scrub herself all over she might also be able to cleanse herself of the guilt that seemed to cling to her like a second skin.

She had dressed again, this time informally in trousers and shaggy sweater, and had loosened her hair and brushed it out until it crackled, then tied it at the back of her neck with a piece of black ribbon. Another firm rat-a-tat on the door made her think Marie had returned, and she ran to open it with a quip on her lips about the so-called punishment—then stopped short in confusion. It wasn't Marie standing there—it was Luke Springer.

CHAPTER TWO

IT WASN'T easy for Jane to look into the brilliant blue eyes beaming down on her without feeling that her guilt was written large on her face. But that initial encounter with Luke was less nerve-racking than she had expected, and mostly because of the warmth of his greeting.

He had shaved and showered, and drips of water from his glistening black hair were falling on to his clean shirt. He shook them off with a laugh—he glowed with good health and vitality, a muscular, bronze giant.

'I'm sorry nobody was at the airport to meet you,' he apologised. 'Carole told me that you caught an earlier flight, and that we must have been fellow passengers. Your face certainly looks familiar—were you the girl in that stunning yellow dress?' He saw Jane blush, and thought that a refreshing change. 'I wish I'd known who you were—I could have offered you a lift,' he added, then frowned, remembering the scene at the airport. 'Perhaps it was just as well,' he said, without explaining why. 'I'm sure you had a more interesting ride on the airport bus, as well as a good tour of St Mary's.'

He looked at his watch. 'We've got half an hour before lunch—would you care for a drink, or shall I ask Marie to make you a coffee?'

At that moment Jane felt that a drink would have a more steadying effect on her nerves than the coffee she would have preferred. 'A sherry, please,' she said in a voice barely more than a whisper, and, with a nod of assent, he led her off to a room at the far end of the corridor.

'What a little thing you are,' he said, looking down at her.
'I hope you won't find the life here too strenuous—but no,
after a city hospital I doubt it. This is my hidey-hole,
retreat, den, office—what have you,' he threw open the door
and they went into a large, square room that in appearance
looked like a library, as three of its walls were lined with
books from floor to ceiling. The fourth was nearly all
window, giving panoramic views of the sea.

It was a comfortable room; someone had made it cosy-
looking with chintz-covered chairs and bowls of flowers.
Flowers of all kinds were plentiful on Scilly—wild flowers
in the fields and on the shore and in hedgerows, and
cultivated flowers wherever there was room for a garden.
Luke walked to the drinks cupboard and poured Jane a
large sherry, then helped himself to whisky and soda and sat
facing her.

After her second gulp of sherry, Jane felt fortified enough
to answer Luke's questions without nervousness, and they
came at her one after another, asked with genuine interest
rather than mere curiosity.

'To get here this early you must have travelled down to
London by the overnight train. Did you find that tiring?'

'I treated myself to a sleeper.'

'The most sensible way to travel at night. Did you sleep
well?' He raised his brows quizzically. 'Some people find
difficulty sleeping on a train—the rocking or the noise keeps
them awake.'

It wasn't the movement or the rhythm of the wheels that
had robbed Jane of sleep—it had been her own conscience.
She said as casually as she could, 'I only slept fitfully, but it
didn't bother me. I read through the guidebook you sent
me.'

Luke looked pleased. 'That was an inspired suggestion on
Carole's part. And what impression did it give you of the
Scillies?'

'It made me feel I knew the islands before I got here, but it didn't prepare me for the pure enchantment I felt as soon as I saw them for myself.'

'Oh, I can see you're hooked.' He laughed. 'And you haven't really seen anything yet—you have quite a treat in store.'

'That's what an old gentleman on the airbus said—well, actually, he said he envied me seeing it all for the first time.'

'Well, I shall be pleased to be the one to show you,' Luke said so naturally that Jane couldn't take it as a personal tribute, yet his words left her with an afterglow of pleasure. 'Is this your first visit to Cornwall?'

Jane admitted it was.

'I suppose you're one of those people who swan off to fabulous foreign places and know nothing about the delights of their own country,' he teased her, and she admitted that, too.

Luke looked at his empty glass and then looked at Jane's, and asked her if she would like another. She shook her head, feeling no longer in need of a stimulant. The first hurdle was over, and Luke wasn't proving the tyrant she had feared. All the same, there was something about him that made her think that his casual, almost indolent manner was only lightly assumed—that underneath that sleepy exterior was a dormant *alter ego* which it would be extremely unwise to arouse. He looked so easy-going and indolent sprawling there in his chair, but she knew that the watchful intelligence for which he was noted never slept.

After a pause, he rose and relieved her of her glass. He didn't immediately resume his chair, but wandered about, jingling the loose change in his pockets—obviously a man who thought better on his feet.

'I was very impressed with your application for this job,' he told her. 'I liked your honest approach. I had many applications from nurses who said they would like to work here on a long-term basis, but on further enquiry I discovered they were only interested in a holiday job. You wanted a holiday job, too, but you were honest enough to say so, and, though I would have preferred someone on a permanent basis, I feel sure you'll tide us over very nicely until then. Another thing in your favour—you trained at St Benedict's. I know Ben from years ago, when I was a house officer there. A very good hospital—anyone they recommend is good enough for me. I assume your nursing officer had no objection to you taking a holiday to help out here?'

Jane remembered the look on the face of Miss Bruce when she had told her how she proposed to spend her annual leave.

'Take a temporary job at a holiday school for deaf children?' she had exclaimed, obviously thinking Jane had also taken temporary leave of her senses. 'Don't we work you hard enough here?' Then her expression had changed, becoming more resigned. 'I suppose there's no rule against it—so long as it doesn't affect your work here afterwards. I can't have one of my staff nurses collapsing on the ward. Why are you doing it—for the money?'

Jane had hesitated before answering. 'In a way,' she had said.

She looked up now to see Luke studying her and, because she couldn't return his gaze without her heart hammering, she stared down at her hands.

'Tell me about yourself,' he said. 'Why did you take up nursing, for instance?'

'My father suggested it—he told me to get myself into a caring profession.'

Luke seemed amused. 'That presupposes you were already in an uncaring profession. Were you?'

Jane realised the ground wasn't so safe, after all—hidden traps appeared in every bend of the conversation. 'I—I was just—well, a sort of office girl,' she said hesitantly, and the words nearly stuck in her throat. Luke made no comment and, gaining confidence, she went on, 'Because of a stroke, my father had become an invalid and needed round-the-clock attention. A woman came in daily to do the housework and cook the meals, and the community nurse called regularly, and then I took over as soon as I came in from work. He was always telling me I should have been a nurse.'

Stephen Peters' actual words had been 'You're far too tender-hearted for the hardbitten world of a newspaper—you should be a nurse. You're a born nurse.' But Jane couldn't tell Luke that, it might have jolted his memory.

'Anyway,' she said, 'I applied to the school of nursing at St Benedict's, and was delighted just as much for my father's sake as for my own that I was accepted as a student, and I qualified last year, just a few weeks before my father died. I was so pleased he lived long enough to know I got my diploma.'

Luke saw the tears gathering on her lashes, and gave her time to recover before saying gently, 'I feel I ought to tell you that I had nearly forty applications for this job. I short-listed them to five, and put you at the top of the list. Would you like to know why?'

Jane did not want to know. She was still too aware that she had come by this job under false pretences, but she had to carry on the charade, so she answered yes.

'Because I felt you wanted this job not because of what it could do for you, but for what *you* could do for the children. Your dedication to children's welfare, especially deprived children, came through so strongly in your letter that it made more impression on me than your qualifications or your references. I could tell you weren't just after a holiday job—you really needed to come to Nightingale House. Am I not right?'

Jane couldn't answer. She hung her head, remembering the sudden emotion that had swept over her when she had written that letter of application. It wasn't the children of Nightingale House she had been thinking of then so much as of Jamie. For her, he was the embodiment of all children handicapped by illness or disability, and in a way her letter had been a cry of protest against their vulnerability.

Watching her, Luke realised that his hunch about this girl had payed off, and, though he had turned down two very suitable applicants, he was glad he had chosen Jane Peters. She would fit in well at Nightingale House, and there was something else about her, too—something that teased his memory. He had seen her somewhere before—apart from on the helicopter that morning—he never forgot a face, and those pool-deep eyes seemed so familiar. Once before dark eyes like that had looked at him with the same mixture of guilt and remorse in their depths, and he wished he could remember where. Who was this girl, and why was he so sure he had met her before—somewhere, some time in the past.

Lunch was a bit of an ordeal, though Luke and Carole did their best to make Jane feel at home. It was their very friendliness that endorsed her guilty feelings; she could have borne such feelings better if the others had been at all condescending or distant towards her, but they were all warmth, and the one who was out in the cold was the girl she had seen at the airport, sitting apart in a cloud of her own disapproval.

When Marie had mentioned someone called Dinah, Jane had assumed she was another domestic. Now she found Marie had been referring to Carole's daughter.

She had changed, or perhaps had been made to change, into a tunic-like dress that made her look more like a schoolgirl. How old was she? Jane wondered—no more than seventeen, perhaps, though she had the appearance of someone older. She sat at the end of the table, picking at her food and darting resentful looks at her mother and Luke and Jane in turn, Jane feeling that the more resentful looks were aimed in her direction. She felt that this mood of childish pique on Dinah's part was not an uncommon occurrence, for the other two treated it with an indifference borne of long practice.

'Our Miss Peters is a dark horse,' said Luke suddenly, and Jane's heart skipped a beat.

'She looks more like a gypsy than a horse,' Jane heard Dinah muttered. If the others heard, they ignored her.

'Are you a dark horse, Jane?' Carole asked as she handed round more salad.

'I—I don't think so.'

'Perhaps calling her a dark horse was too strong,' Luke said on reflection. 'I meant she has hidden depths. Carole, do you know she cared for her invalid father until he died, and she was training to be a nurse at the same time? That must have taken some stamina.'

'There was just you and your father?' Carole asked sympathetically.

'I have an older sister, but she was married and living in Devon at the time, and my mother died when I was a child.' Jane began to feel uncomfortable. Luke had made her out to be some kind of a paragon, which she certainly was not. 'I didn't do any more for my father than he did for me when I was young,' she said feebly.

'And modest with it,' Dinah muttered sarcastically, and Jane saw Luke's lips tighten.

Diplomatically, she said,

'What are my duties, exactly? I mean, will I be doing any actual nursing? There doesn't seem enough for me to do——'

Luke cut in with a chuckle. 'I'll see to it that you'll have enough to do. I can be a hard taskmaster—ask Carole. As for nursing—not in any serious way, I hope. Earlier on in the year we had a child here with asthma, and, believe me, I could have done with a nurse to help me then. So when I realised I should have to take on another helper, I thought it would be best all round to have someone with nursing experience, if not a fully qualified nurse. This job would have suited an older, semi-retired woman—but I'm glad we got you instead.'

There came a snort from the end of the table. Jane had an uncontrollable urge to giggle, but dared not, as Luke looked annoyed. He turned his attention to her again.

'Your first priority will be to learn how to communicate with the children. It's a lot to ask of you in the short time you'll be here, but the children themselves will more than meet you half-way—they're very quick. Your main duties will be to look after their welfare—bath and dress the younger ones, round them up for meals, supervise their playtime, things like that. Don't worry, we'll find plenty for you do do.' His smile was more of a promise than a threat.

When lunch was over, Carole took Jane on a tour of the house. First of all to the kitchen, where Marie was washing the dishes, assisted by two of the older girls. The younger children were having their afternoon rest, which accounted, Carole explained with a smile, for the unnatural quiet.

Next Jane was shown the children's playroom—a beautifully appointed room with high windows that had originally been a billiards room. Then on to the room that Carole called the family living-room—a homely, spacious, lived-in room with plenty of well-used chairs and sofas, coffee-tables, footstools, cushions, magazine racks and flowers. It was a house of flowers. Apart from a grand piano, there was nothing here to spoil—no valuable rugs or ornaments. It reminded Jane of the lounge of a country hotel, and that was exactly what it had been, Carole told her.

'This was the residents' lounge when this place was a hotel—you can see the lovely views there are from here—right across to Tresco and Samson. The furniture looks a bit shabby, and we could do with a set of new loose covers, but they'll have to wait. We come here to unwind at the end of the day—and do I look forward to that! Especially when Dinah has been more tiresome than usual. I must apologise for her behaviour at the lunch-table; I could have shaken her!'

'I don't want people to be on their best behaviour just for me,' said Jane, for the want of something to say.

Carole looked at her. 'I'm afraid that *was* Dinah's best behaviour,' she said wryly, then changed the subject.

'That's all I can show you of the house at present. I'd like to show you where we sleep the children, but they're resting—or supposed to be—at the moment. There's no television in here, you notice, but there's a set in the drawing-room upstairs—that's such a stiff and formal room, we rarely use it. If we're desperate for television, we crowd into the kitchen and watch on the portable set we bought for Marie—she doesn't mind.'

Recalling the size of the kitchen, Jane didn't think there was much danger of crowding. Her eye roved over the family photgraphs displayed on the high mantelpiece, among which was a photo of three schoolboys—two the same sage, one some years younger, and all looking like young editions of Luke Springer. Seeing her looking at it, Carole reached it down.

'It's a photo of my husband and his two brothers—you can tell they're brothers, can't you? They all have the same black curly hair and the Springer eyes. That's Luke,' she said, pointing to the one in the middle, 'and that's Edward, my husband, on the left. Ned and Luke look like twins,

don't they? Actually there were eighteen months between
them. Ned, then Luke, then Robin, the baby.' She replaced
the photo, drawing her fingers gently across the likeness of
the boy who had been her husband. 'Ned died six years
ago,' she said. 'Nothing—nobody has ever filled the gap.'
She drew a shaky breath. 'It's helped me, coming
here—making myself useful—but then again, it's caused
other problems—with Dinah.'

Carole hesitated, seeming to have some inner tussle
which she resolved by suddenly unburdening herself to
Jane.

'I honestly don't know what to do about that girl. Her
father spoiled her—no, it's not fair to lay all the blame on
poor Ned—I spoiled her just as much as he did, but Dinah
idolised him. He died when she was ten, and that did
something to her. She had always been a wilful child, but
after Ned died she became unmanageable, and I couldn't
cope—not at that time. I sent her away to school, thinking it
was best for both of us, but I realise no   hat it was a
dreadful mistake on my part. First Dinah lost her father,
then she thought I'd rejected her. She's been expelled from
five different schools—the last one at Christmas. I don't
know what to do about her—I thought bringing her here to
Nightingale House might help solve the problem, but if
anything it's created more problems. Neither of us has seen
much of Luke in the past few years, as he'd been living
abroad. Then he came back into our lives again, looking so
much like Ned it was—well, a bit of a shock to us, especially
to Dinah. Every time she looks at him she sees her
father—in some ways he *is* her father, and she hangs around
him as if fearful of letting him out of her sight, and is
terribly resentful of anyone else he takes notice of. She's
become so possessive with him that she's making a pest of
herself. Luke is very good with her, he makes
allowances—but even he loses his patience at times. I'll

just have to start looking around for another school—that is, if I can find one that will take her.

'That business at the airport, Luke told me about that—the spectacle she made of herself in that tight sweater and cut-off jeans. She does it to show off—to get attention. She's still a child at heart, and she doesn't know when she oversteps the mark. For instance—taking the car like that without permission. She thinks she can get away with anything on this island, but the rules apply here just as much as they do on the mainland—taking a risk like that, the little idiot!'

'She hasn't passed her test, then?'

'Passed her test?' Carole's voice rose. 'She isn't even old enough to take driving lessons—she's not seventeen yet.' Carole gave a helpless sigh. 'She's so much like her father in some ways—absolutely irresponsible, but that was one of the things I loved about him, so I shouldn't be grumbling, should I? I remember my mother-in-law telling me that her three boys were known as the adventurous one, the clever one, and the musical one. You can guess who the clever one is, that's Luke, and Robin—poor Robin, he was the musical one. And my Ned, my fearless Ned—he didn't care a damn about anything—except perhaps his wife and daughter.' Her eyes filled with tears. 'Those three brothers,' she said. 'So alike in looks, and so different in personality—what a pity their faults and good points couldn't have been distributed a little more evenly between them.' Another sigh. 'And now, of the three, only Luke is left, and if he doesn't marry—and so far he's shown no inclination to do so—the family name will die out.'

This left many questions hanging in the air—had Robin been married, for instance? And why *poor* Robin? Carole had not referred to poor Ned, though both were dead, presumably—but they were not questions Jane could have asked.

In spite of all her misgivings, Jane slept well that night. She had spent the afternoon and the evening familiarising herself with the children and learning their names. Luke had given her some booklets on the causes and treatment of deafness, and another booklet explaining about sign language, with suitable illustrations. This was something she would have to learn if she wanted to communicate with the children, and she put the books aside to study later.

One thing surprised her about the children—the amount of noise they made.

'That's because they can't hear themselves,' Luke explained, adding with a smile, 'Try plugging your ears with cotton wool, then stamp your feet—you won't hear yourself, or very faintly, if you do. These kids don't realise the noise they make. How can they? But you'll get so used to stamping feet and slamming doors, and the banging and the shouting that goes on, you won't notice it in time.'

Time—what time? Jane asked herself. A month—and she shivered inwardly, knowing what Roy expected of her during that month.

The group of children staying at Nightingale House at present ranged in ages from seven to eleven. Each group stayed for two weeks, and the present lot of children had one more week to go before another group took over.

'So the children never stay long enough for you to get to know them really well,' she said, thinking of Becky.

'This is a holiday home, not a school,' Luke reminded her. 'And we must always remain impartial, never become too fond of any one child—that way danger lies.' Jane thought that an odd thing for him to say, and again thought of Becky. It would be easy to become fond of such a winning child; she knew she could easily do so herself.

She said, 'I haven't seen Becky for the past hour. She isn't with the others.'

'She's inclined to wander off on her own, but don't

worry, she can't get out of the grounds. She'll turn up when she's hungry.' Luke seemed unconcerned, and Jane went off to get the children ready for supper. As Becky still hadn't put in an appearance, she volunteered to go and look for her.

There were many places in the gardens that made ideal hidey-holes for children—particularly around the carn, as a gap between two of the boulders made a favourite spot for playing in. But Becky wasn't there, nor in the old stables, nor in that part of the garden that had been made into a playground with swings and slides and a see-saw.

Jane finally ran her to earth in the shrubbery, the last place she had expected to find her, as it was shadowy and damp and the haunt of spiders. Becky was crouched under one of the bushes, hugging her teddy and crying—a soundless weeping that went to Jane's heart.

She saw at once what the trouble was—the shapeless old bear had lost its smaller companion. The string that held them together had come undone, and was trailing from the bigger bear's neck. Jane squatted on the ground, wondering how she could find out from this tearful child how she had come to lose the smaller bear—where had she been with it, for instance? She didn't think she could make herself understood, but she had reckoned without Becky's resourcefulness, as she quickly realised what Jane wanted of her. She scrambled to her feet and, indicating to Jane to follow her, led her a merry dance deep into the shrubbery, until the evergreen bushes became so dense there was only one way to get through them, and that was to go down on one's hands and knees and crawl under the lowest branches. This Becky did, grinning over her shoulder to see if Jane was following suit—for her, the search had turned into something of a game.

At least Jane spotted the lost teddy—it was caught up on one of the spines of a gorse bush. Why Becky should have crawled into such an unlikely place to play in the first place was a mystery Jane knew she would never solve. It was enough for her that Becky was happy again; the look on her face when Jane held the lost bear aloft was radiant.

But Jane got her reward. They had battled their way back to the clearing and were resting when Becky shyly coiled her arms around Jane's neck and kissed her. Jane found herself clasping the thin little body close to her, and burying her face in the child's hair. Then—this was no time for sentimentality, she thought, checking her tears. She mustn't allow memories of Jamie to take over. With an effort, she drew away.

'And now,' she said, speaking slowly and distinctly so that Becky could understand. Jane suspected that Becky could lip-read—which she could, up to a point. 'We must see to it that Mummy Teddy doesn't lose her baby again, so I'll show you how to tie a knot that won't come undone.'

They were intent on this when Luke came looking for them—and found them sitting side by side on a hummock of grass, absorbed in doing something together.

Luke looked Jane up and down, unable to conceal his amusement. Bits of turf and leaves were stuck to her hair, her sweater was marked with earth stains, and there were damp patches on the knees of her jeans. Unperturbed, Jane explained what had happened, adding, 'And they shouldn't come adrift again, as I've shown Becky how to tie a reef knot. She's very quick—I only had to show her once.'

Luke chuckled. 'You both look as if you've been excavating—looking for another burial ground, perhaps? Did you know there are ancient burial grounds on Scilly? Here, let me help you up.' He pulled Jane to her feet. 'Thank you for going to all that trouble for Becky—I'm afraid it's ruined your jeans.'

She looked down and for the first time noticed the stains. What a sight you look, she thought, unaware that Luke was looking at her as if the sight he saw gave him much pleasure.

How had she ever come to think this man was cold and arrogant? she wondered, for the eyes that she had thought of as frosty were tender-looking, even wistful, as he gazed thoughtfully at little Becky. He swooped on her and tossed her in the air before putting her on his shoulders to give her a 'flying angel' back to the house, and she clung to his hair for support, showing her joy at this unusual mode of travel, not with squeals of delight, which were beyond her, but with a broad smile and eyes that expressed her feelings.

Jane was more than ever struck by the likeness between them. In spite of Carole's denial of any relationship, Jane was convinced that Becky was Luke's daughter—a conviction that made her only too aware of a sudden little ache in the region of her heart.

She was awakened early the following morning by a shaft of sunlight falling across her pillow. She had opened the curtains before putting out the light, and now she lay looking out at the tops of the trees and the sea beyond. The garden was full of birdsong, and a blackbird near the open window was singing at full volume. She could pick out a thrush and a chaffinch amid the medley, and, from the direction of the coast, the evocative call of a cuckoo. But nearly drowning the liquid notes of the songbirds was the mewing of the seagulls as they swooped in from the sea and circled around the house before finding a foothold on the roof. Once landed, they kept up a continuous squawking, and made so much noise that any chance of her dozing off again was out of the question. Jane had just made up her mind to shower and dress and go for a walk before breakfast when she saw the handle of her door slowly turning.

She sat up in bed, wondering who could be stealing in upon her at such an early hour. The handle turned fully, the door opened a crack—then a little wider, and a pair of smiling blue eyes peered in at her. It was Becky, barefoot and in her nightie, and carrying, not a teddy this time, but an equally disreputable-looking toy pig.

She pattered across the floor and climbed in with Jane, snuggling down beside her. She had another smaller knitted pig tucked under her arm and it wasn't necessary for her to sign what it was she had come for, Jane guessed. Becky wanted the pig and piglet tied together.

The last thing Jane had thought to bring with her was a ball of string, but, not wanting to disappoint Becky, she racked her brains to think what she could use as an alternative. She could cut some shoulder-straps from her undies—they were easily replaceable, and it was worth a small sacrifice just to see Becky's face light up again. Jane got out of bed, found her nail scissors, and snipped off the shoulder-straps from her one and only full-length slip. In the meantime an expectant small girl watched every move she made with studied attention.

Jane tied the two pigs together in the way she had earlier shown Becky—they made a bulky, unmanageable armful, but Becky was delighted. Not forgetting her duty, she rewarded Jane with another kiss, then climbed down from the bed and, hugging the pigs close to her, slipped away as quietly as she had come.

Why this compulsion to tie like and like together? Jane wondered. Why this enacting the role of mother and baby, and the obvious fear of them ever becoming separated? Was Becky trying to say something about her own short past—had she ever been parted from her mother? Jane sighed, curious about that absent mother. In her dressing-gown, she went over to the window and stared out with dreaming eyes at the crystal-clear sea. The atmosphere was so free from pollution that visibility was possible for several miles.

Tresco and Bryher and Samson floated on the waters like a pattern of islands, and beyond them was a group of rocks, majestic but treacherous.

The air felt as soft as silk against her skin—if she had this weather for the whole of her stay, it would be the holiday of a lifetime. Then reality hit her like a blow. Holiday—this was no holiday, this was a campaign of deception, and the image of Roy Barford's foxlike face blotted everything else from her mind.

Marie rescued her from troubled thoughts by suddenly appearing with early morning tea. 'I guessed you'd be awake,' she said. 'I knew those gulls wouldn't give you any peace. I'll soon shut them up.' She put the cup on the bedside-table and, rushing to the window, leant out as far as she could. 'Shut up, you noisy brutes, I'll see to you in a minute!' she bellowed, making so much noise herself that Jane felt sure she would arouse the entire household.

The gulls took flight, but as soon as Marie withdrew her head they were back, and screeching as much as ever.

'It's no good,' said Marie resigned. 'I'd better go down and feed them. There won't be any peace until I do—my own fault for starting it in the first place——'

'Marie,' said Jane impulsively, not stopping to choose her words. 'Is little Becky one of the family?'

Marie pursed her lips with disapproval—talk she could, and often did, but she never indulged in gossip. 'All the children are one family while under this roof,' she said primly. 'The doctor makes no exceptions.'

Jane looked so crestfallen that Marie relented. 'Well, I suppose Becky is kind of special,' she conceded, but with some reluctance. 'For one thing, she isn't like the rest of the children here—she's dumb as well as deaf. The others can all make some kind of noise—you've heard them—but not Becky. Perhaps that's why . . .' Marie hesitated. 'It's not for me to say, but I can't help wondering if that's why she's here as a permanent guest—the doctor keeping an eye on her, if you know what I mean.'

'Then she isn't on an extended holiday?'

'Oh, no, she was here before I came, and that was just after Christmas. And it's a funny thing—if she has got a family, none of them ever come to visit her—or write or send her presents. Not that she goes short of anything, Dr Springer sees to that.'

'I wonder,' Jane mused, her dark eyes thoughtful. 'This obsession she has with tying two toys together as if one were the mother and the other the child—I wonder if there's any significance in that. Children do act out their fears and fancies in play.'

'I wouldn't know anything about that,' answered Marie shortly, feeling out of her depth—feeling, too, that she had betrayed a confidence. She liked Miss Peters very much, but felt now that she was showing too much curiosity about the private life of the doctor. Marie would have defended Dr Springer with her life if necessary.

'I must go down and start the breakfasts,' she said, making purposefully towards the door. 'Before I know where I am I'll have a horde of hungry youngsters descending upon me.'

'I'll be down as soon as possible to help,' Jane promised, gulping down the rest of her tea. She showered and dressed. The jeans she had worn the day before would have to go to the cleaners—so, too, would the yellow dress she had travelled in, for that had got soiled on the journey. She put on her faded jeans, the only other pair she had with her, and with them a striped green and blue top. She was in too much of a hurry to bother much with her hair, so she left it hanging loose, fastening it back from her face with a hair-grip.

She was downstairs before the children, but not before Luke; she met him in the hall, and noticed he was carrying a pair of sea-boots.

'I've just been listening to the weather forecast,' he said. 'This fine spell is coming to an end shortly. I thought we'd make the most of it and take the kids out on a picnic. Samson would be an ideal spot on a day like this.'

'Samson—the uninhabited island? How do we get there?'

Luke laughed. 'By boat, of course—unless you'd rather swim!' He was in a teasing mood, his blue eyes dancing.

Jane's face fell. 'I'm not a very good sailor——'

'You don't have to be today—you're only a passenger, and the sea is as calm as a lake, so you'll have nothing to fear. It's all in the mind, anyway.'

Before Jane had a chance to challenge that statement, the phone on the hall-table rang. Luke answered it, then called after her as she walked on towards the kitchen. 'It's for you, and it's urgent—someone calling from London. Would you like to take it in my study—it'll be more private?'

Privacy was the last thing on Jane's mind at that moment. An urgent call from London meant only one thing—something had happened to Jamie! Trembling inwardly, she took the receiver from Luke, and a familiar nasal voice came over the phone.

'Hello, ducky. So you did arrive safely, after all—I thought perhaps you'd got lost!' There was a barbed undertone to the caller's humour. 'And what happened about your promise to phone me? You didn't forget your old pal Roy, did you?'

CHAPTER THREE

LUKE headed for the stairs like a man in a hurry. Jane waited until he was out of earshot before speaking into the earpiece in a feverish whisper.

'This is not a convenient time for me to talk—I'm just about to give the children their breakfast——'

Roy brushed that excuse aside, and she could picture him, his lip curled and a cigar between his fingers. 'If you'd called me last night, as arranged, there would be no need for me to bother you now. What news have you got for me—hard news, I mean?'

Jane swallowed back her revulsion. 'I've hardly been here twenty-four hours—what do you expect me to find out in that time? Nothing has happened here yet—nothing at all.'

'Of course nothing's happened—you've got to make things happen.' Roy sounded impatient. 'I'm not paying you to sit around enjoying yourself, ducky. I want you to get down to business. Have you located Springer's office yet—his desk where he keeps his private things, that kind of thing—or a safe, even? Have you seen a safe anywhere?'

Jane felt her blood pressure dropping—a feeling of nausea and dizziness, a sense of consciousness draining away. She took several deep breaths—she mustn't let Roy have this effect on her. She mustn't! 'You haven't told me what it is I'm supposed to be looking for,' she parried.

'Ye gods! I've been over this a dozen times. Anything that will incriminate him—anything to give us a clue as to why he left his job with the Home Office——'

Jane took a grip on herself. 'What's this talk of

incrimination—why should you think Dr Springer has anything to hide? And another thing,' she warmed up to her subject, 'you told me he'd relinquished his title of doctor—that isn't true, is it? Everybody here refers to him as Doctor, and I can easily check for myself whether he's still on the medical register—there's a copy here in the library.'

There was a moment's pause, then she heard Roy chuckle—a chuckle that was more sinister than humorous. 'All right, I did bend the truth a little,' he admitted. 'I thought if I told you Springer was now a plain mister you wouldn't have the same qualms about spying on him as you would if he were a doctor—knowing the hallowed respect you nurses have for doctors! No harm done, I knew you'd find out, anyway—but by then it would be too late for you to do anything about it.'

'It's not too late for me to walk out,' Jane answered with spirit, but she knew she couldn't do that, and not only because of Jamie.

'It is too late, ducky.' Roy's nasal laugh grated on her ears. 'And you know it. Now what are your plans for today?'

He listened without interruption while Jane told him, then said, 'Well, I suppose it could be worse. I'd rather you were in the house, looking around for some evidence, but the next best thing is to be alone with him on a romantic island. Lay on the charm as thickly as possible, and see what you can get out of him—it shouldn't be difficult, he's a man and you're an attractive young girl. Today's Sunday. I'll give you until Wednesday, and you'd better find out something for me by then.'

'If there is anything to find out,' Jane said meaningfully.

'There will be, ducky. I always make sure before staking my money. Bye now, and happy sleuthing.'

He could have spared me that last, Jane thought bitterly

as she replaced the receiver. She felt sick to the core of her being, and tears of frustration started to her eyes. Looking up, she saw Dinah standing on the bottom stair, watching her. Could she have been there long? Could she have overheard?

'Having trouble with the boyfriend?' Dinah asked, smirking. It was the first time she had spoken to Jane.

'It wasn't my boyfriend!'

'Oh, sorry—I thought it was, by the way you were whispering so furtively.'

'It was nobody important,' Jane answered wearily, and Dinah shrugged, then walked off down the hall with an exaggerated roll of her hips. This morning she was wearing her hair in a different style—she had scraped it to the top of her head and tethered it in such a way that it sprouted out like a fountain. She had on a pair of tight-fitting cropped trousers the colour of ripe tomatoes, and over them a loose white shirt showing three inches of cleavage. Jane sighed, giving a thought for Carole's feelings, knowing that Dinah was deliberately setting out to provoke her mother.

Sunday was truly a day of rest for Marie; it was her one day off in the week, and she spent it with friends in Hugh Town. As soon as the breakfast dishes were washed-up—and, though there was a gleaming, up-to-date dishwasher sitting in the corner of the kitchen, she preferred to do her pots and pans by the time-hallowed method of scouring pad and elbow grease—she changed into her worsted suit and silk blouse, and set off on her bike with a large bunch of sweet-williams tied to the handlebars.

Carole did the cooking on Sundays. 'I hope you don't mind coming back to an all-fish supper?' she asked Jane. 'Marie can't stand the smell of fish, so I always take the opportunity to try out a fish dish when she's away, especially as the seas around here are teaming with fish of all varieties.'

'I could live on fish,' Jane answered, which was true—she wasn't a big meat eater.

Part of the stable block was now used as garages, which, besides the sports car which had fetched Luke from the airport, gave house-room to an elderly minibus, a small sailing-boat and an inflatable dinghy. Jane looked askance at the last.

'Are we sailing to Samson in either of those?' she asked anxiously of Luke.

He gave a deep chuckle. 'No—I don't think they're quite up to carrying twelve of us. I've left our old butty down on the shore. I got up early this morning and fetched her in from her mooring.'

It was quite a feat rounding up the excited children—one or other of them would suddenly remember they had left some crucial object behind and would run back for it. What with the food hampers which Carole and Marie had provided, the assortment of spades and pails, balls, bats, skipping ropes, etcetera, it was quite a tight fit in the bus. Once they were all aboard, Luke clapped his hands to get their attention. Those who could not hear—a few of the children had a little hearing and wore hearing-aids—felt the vibration. 'Right,' he said. 'Now, are you all carrying your own towels and swimsuits?' and he held his aloft to show them. They responded by joyfully waving theirs in return.

'I thought the seas were too cold for bathing in the Scillies, even in high summer,' Jane queried.

'They are—but you try keeping these children out of the water—especially with the sun shining. I don't relish going for a dip this time of the year, but there's very little difference in the temperature of the waters around these islands between summer and winter. Do you swim?'

Jane shook her head. 'I don't like being in the water any more than I like being on it,' she answered candidly.

Luke laughed. 'We'll soon cure you of that phobia.' He

counted heads. 'We all seem to be aboard, so let's go.'

Jane had also been counting heads. 'I don't see Becky. Isn't she coming with us?'

'No, she's staying behind with Carole and Dinah. She's been to Samson before, and, as you saw for yourself yesterday, she's got a habit of wandering off. When we go off in a crowd like this, it's one person's work to keep an eye on her. If Dinah had been coming——' He broke off, his face registering annoyance. 'I was hoping she'd come along, as she's good with the children, though you might not believe it after the way she behaved yesterday. But she didn't want to come; she said she'd already made her plans. She was just being awkward—another time I wouldn't be able to get rid of her.'

Luke negotiated the narrow bend out of the lane on to the road, and the subject of Dinah was dropped. They passed a couple of hikers, and this prompted Luke to remark, 'There are some jolly fine walks on St Mary's. The island is only three miles wide, but it's nine miles following the coastline—a nice easy day's stroll at this time of year, and a paradise for ornithologists and, of course, botanists. Are you interested in nature?'

'At St Benedict's I had more opportunity to study human nature than the kind you mean,' said Jane, smiling.

'Well, you must make the most of it while you're here.' Luke gave her a sideways look. 'Perhaps we can persuade you to stay longer—perhaps the Scillies will work a magic spell on you, so that you won't be able to leave,' and, though he was joking, Jane felt an undercurrent of earnestness in his voice.

They turned off the road and along a narrow track that descended across moorland and led to a small bay tucked in between two granite headlands. Luke parked the minibus, and then it was just a short scramble across a shingle bar that separated the moor from the fine shell-white sands of the bay.

It was easier to walk on the sand barefoot, and Jane followed the children's example and slipped off her sandals. The younger children were left to amuse themselves while the older ones helped ferry the goods from the bus to the large wooden boat pulled up on the foreshore.

'Is that what you call a butty?' asked Jane when the boat was finally loaded.

'It's what *I* call a butty,' Luke explained. 'Mostly because we only use it for picnicking on other islands. I think it was once a yacht's tender. It's a heavy old craft, but practically unsinkable. For pootling about in the bay I use the dinghy or the sail-boat. All aboard? I want two hefty volunteers to help me push the boat out.' He tapped two of the bigger boys on their shoulders. 'You, Tom, and you, Nigel.'

The butty had a powerful outboard motor, and they were beaching on Samson in a little under thirty minutes. The short trip had been uneventful, as the water was as smooth as silk, and Jane's main worry was not about feeling queasy, but seeing that the children didn't fall overboard. Most of them were hanging over the side of the boat, trailing their hands in the water, and keeping a hold on limbs or clothes kept Jane fully occupied, so the relief she felt when she heard the keel scraping on the sand wasn't entirely on her own account.

As soon as the children were lifted out on to the shore they scattered. 'It's all right,' said Luke, seeing Jane looking after them apprehensively. 'Tracy and Karen are in charge. They're sensible girls, and will keep the young ones in order. Help me unload this gear, and then we'll organise some amusements.'

The children soon changed out of their clothes and were running about in swimwear. Luke disappeared behind some crags, and when he reappeared he, too, was in swimming trunks. 'What about you?' he asked Jane. 'Aren't you going to change?'

'I haven't got a swimsuit.'

'What a lame excuse—you could have borrowed one from Carole.' He waded out as far as his shins, then grinned back over his shoulder. 'You're better off there, anyway—excuse my language, but the water is so bloody cold!'

The children didn't seem to notice the cold—they ran in and out of the waves like the tiny wading birds that darted about along the tideline. Luke wasn't in there with them for his own enjoyment, just to keep an eye on them in case they got into danger. He looked larger than life in swimwear. The muscles in his arms stood out like steel ropes, and Jane, baffled by an unexpected surge of emotion, looked away in embarrassment.

Afterwards he lay full-length on a towel, drying himself in the sun. Little droplets of water glistened among the hairs of his chest, and Jane, who had always been repelled by the idea of hairy men, now found Luke's hairiness attractive. It was part of his strength and masculinity, as in biblical times it had been Samson's—and she smiled to herself for comparing Luke with Samson on this island called Samson. It was an unfortunate analogy, because immediately her mind leapt to Delilah, who had betrayed him—and that was too near the bone for comfort.

The smaller children came to her to be rubbed down and dressed. Luke had turned over and was sunning his back, his head pillowed in his arms. His long lashes curved on his cheek, and she thought he had gone to sleep, until she saw a gleam of blue and realised he was watching her through half-closed eyelids.

'You do that with a very practised air,' he drawled. 'Were you on the children's ward at St Benedict's?'

'For a time—I also have a young nephew——' It was out before she could stop herself, and she had hoped to avoid any mention of Jamie.

Luke sat up, brushing the sand off his arms. He sat forward, his arms folded across his chest, regarding her. 'I know nothing about your family—apart from your father. For all I know you might be married——'

'I'm not,' she said with a laugh.

'Engaged or attached?' He raised his brows enquiringly.

'Neither.'

'Good.' He made no effort to conceal his pleasure. 'Well, let's get these kids to work—get them to work up an appetite for their lunch.'

Getting them to work meant organising a game of rounders, followed by cricket—and then, for the younger ones, hide and seek. There were plenty of places to hide in—no trees, but jungles of briar and bramble and inches-high green bracken, and great granite boulders. Just before midday the deep boom of a ship's siren sounded over the water.

'What was that?' cried Jane, startled.

'Only the *Scillonian* announcing its arrival.' Luke took her by her shoulders and turned her to face the sea. 'Watch, and you'll see her coming through Crow Sound—there, you can see her now—isn't that a fine sight?' His eyes gleamed appreciatively. 'She's more than a ferry, she's our lifeline to the mainland. Everything we use on Scilly—food, milk, coal, furniture, cars—everything you see in the shop windows—the papers, magazines, books, some of the mail—it all comes on the *Scillonian*. I'd forgotten she was sailing today—she doesn't sail every Sunday. She docks about midday, so now is as good a time as any to start unpacking those hampers.'

While Jane, with help from Tracy and Karen, laid the tablecloth which they had spread on a level stretch of grass, Luke went off to find somewhere to dress—not so easy now that one of the pleasure boats had dropped off half a dozen of its passengers on the island.

Samson was small, but there was still room to wander out of sight of one another, and it was these wanderers that Luke kept a look-out for as he struggled into his clothes behind the shelter of a granite boulder. When he returned to his party, Jane was cutting up large Cornish pasties and passing them round on paper plates to the children.

'This is more like it,' Luke said appreciatively. 'I'm glad we're picnicking up here and not on the beach; I don't care much for sandy sandwiches.'

Jane had positioned herself between Tracy and a small boy with spiky white-gold hair. Luke bodily picked up the boy—who didn't stop eating—and put him down again several places along. '*I* sit at the head of the table,' he said with a grin, easing his long length down beside Jane.

The children were quiet during the meal, one or two of the youngest already drooping over their plates. The combination of fresh air, exercise and excitement was taking its toll, and when the eating was over it didn't take much persuasion to get them to lie down in the shade and sleep. Even the two older girls were glad to sit quietly.

'I was hoping to take you on a short exploration of the island,' Luke said as he helped Jane repack the remains of the meal. 'Perhaps we'll have time when the children wake up. Are you quite happy sitting here awhile?'

'I can't think of anything I'd rather be doing,' Jane replied in all honesty. She was sitting with her back against one of the rocks, looking towards St Mary's. The harbour looked as blue as in a child's painting, and with the help of Luke's binoculars she could pick out the landmarks he pointed out to her—Star Castle, Buzza Tower, Carn Thomas towering above the lifeboat station, and Peninnis Lighthouse—places she had been told of or read about.

'It's so peaceful here,' she said. 'It's hard to describe—perhaps tranquil is the nearest I can get to it.'

'Tranquil—yes, that's a good word,' Luke said musingly.

'Scilly is tranquil—and restful.' He lay on his side on the grass, propped up on one elbow. 'That sense of tranquillity is what attracted me to it in the first place. Time doesn't matter on Scilly—not for some of us.'

Jane felt her pulse quicken. She remembered Roy's words on the phone—'I'd rather you were in the house, looking around for some evidence, but the next best thing is to be alone with him on a romantic island.' Well, she *was* alone with him, for the sleeping children didn't count, and what could be more romantic than this setting of blue seas and golden sands, with gulls, their wings silvered by the sun, floating effortlessly above them, and a carpet of pink sea-thrift scenting the ground round about? Yes, what could be a more romantic place for a spot of treachery? she asked herself savagely, and Luke wondered at the sudden shudder that went through her.

He sat up. 'Have you got chilled? Would you like my jersey to put around your shoulders?'

She gave a faint smile. 'I'm not cold—it was just that somebody walked over my grave.' An image of Jamie came to her mind—Jamie as he was, Jamie as he could be again, and her determination hardened. 'Did you know the Scillies at all before you came here?' And with that simple question she put her scruples behind her.

Not that she had to do much probing—Luke seemed to want to talk, to tell her what, after a long quest, had brought him to St Mary's and Nightingale House.

'I'd been looking around for a suitable place to turn into a holiday home for deaf children—near to the sea and fairly accessible to shops etcetera, yet away from the busy watering-places that in summer become congested with holiday-makers, and in the south-west if possible because of the milder climate.

'I'd looked at other places in Cornwall, but I hadn't given a thought to Scilly. Then in an estate agent's in Penzance

I saw that a one-time hotel on St Mary's was for sale; the price was right, the size was right, so I came over to view it. And the minute I stepped off the *Scillonian* I was hooked—I stood there looking around me and, though it was a cold grey misty kind of day and everywhere looked out of focus, I knew without doubt that my search was over. Have you ever had that kind of conviction about something or someone?'

'Yes,' said Jane, remembering the man with fearless blue eyes on the steps of the Old Bailey.

'Then you know how I felt. Everything else slotted into place. The house was in good condition—it didn't need much doing to it. It had already been arranged that Carole would come as my housekeeper. I took a few months to settle in before I started to plan for the children's visits—the first one was this Easter. Marie came to us just after Christmas—one of the hoteliers in Hugh Town recommended her. I did have a part-time secretary for a little while—a local girl, who was glad of the work, for there isn't much work for the young of Scilly out of season—but then the opportunity came for a suitable job on the mainland, and she took it. I haven't the need for many secretarial duties, but, as you once worked in an office, perhaps you wouldn't mind——'

'Any time,' Jane finished for him. 'My shorthand is a bit rusty, but I've kept up my typing.'

He gave her a quizzical look. 'You're quite a girl, aren't you? A secretary, a nurse—is there anything else I should know about you?'

Jane shook her head. 'I'm very ordinary, really. I'm just someone who started out with shorthand and typing and finished up with a nursing diploma instead. I changed horses in midstream, and did myself a favour. I love nursing.'

'What about your family?'

'There's only my sister and myself now. We share a house in Surrey—old and shabby, but comfortable, where we were born——'

'Is that the married sister you mentioned yesterday—the one who lives in Devon?'

A flicker of a shadow crossed Jane's face. She said, 'She used to live in Devon. Susan and Jim, her husband, had a bee in their bonnet about farming, and, though Jim had a good job as an accountant, he gave it up and they moved down to Devon, but the farm didn't pay. Everything went wrong for them.' Her voice was so low, Luke could hardly hear her. 'Then they were involved in a car crash . . . Anyway, when my father died they sold up and moved in with me. Jim has gone back to accountancy and works at home now.'

'Was it your brother-in-law who phoned you this morning?'

'No, it—it was someone else.'

Luke looked at her so hard that Jane felt her colour rising. 'So it *was* a boyfriend this morning?'

'I have no boyfriend,' said Jane, more emphatically that she intended, and Luke flashed her a questioning look.

'Well, if it wasn't a boyfriend, it was someone who thinks very highly of you, to phone you before eight-thirty on a Sunday.' He turned away, his profile outlined against the sky. He had a strong chin which, in certain moods, gave him a look of arrogance. Jane had experienced that arrogance on their first ill-starred meeting, but there had been no signs of it since. He seemed a much softer and more approachable man than he had five years ago—and yet she couldn't rid herself of a feeling that there was something in his past that haunted him. Roy had put the idea into her mind in the first place, and since her arrival at Nightingale House she had seen Luke on two occasions lapse into another world, losing himself in uneasy thoughts that changed the whole aspect of his countenance, giving him almost a look of melancholia. Then, just as quickly, he had snapped out of it and whatever it was that had stirred up such unpleasant associations, he managed to brush aside. Today, so far, there had been no sudden change of mood.

He said, taking her unawares, 'Has it struck you what a coincidence it is that you should be working at Nightingale House?'

A warning bell sounded in Jane's head, and her heart beat faster. 'A c-coincidence?'

'Very much so. A nightingale living in a house called Nightingale—get it?' He laughed, and Jane exhaled a long sigh of relief.

'Oh, you mean *that* kind of nightingale—the connection with Florence Nightingale. How did Nightingale House come by its name? I did wonder. Do nightingales sing in the garden?'

Luke was sceptical. 'I doubt it—not these days, anyway. I've yet to meet anybody who's heard a nightingale singing on Scilly, though it's a stopping-off place for migrant birds. But there is a tale attached to the house, if you'd like to hear it?'

She could have listened to his voice for hours—it was deep and mellifluous.

'Well, it appears that some time int he 1840s a young seaman from Scilly set off to America to make his fortune. He got caught up in the 1848 gold rush of California, and was one of the few to strike lucky. A few years later he returned to St Mary's to marry his childhood sweetheart, and told her he'd build her a house anywhere she liked on the island. Then she reminded him that once during their courting days they had heard a nightingale singing—she could remember the very spot, and she wanted her house built there. So that's what the young man did, and they called it Nightingale House. I can't vouch for the truth of that legend, but it makes a nice story. A good selling point, too, the estate agent told me.'

'Now you've spoiled a lovely story by being cynical. I believe it because I want to believe it—it's so romantic.'

'You believe in romance?'

'Yes.' Jane was emphatic about that. 'We need romance to help us face up to reality.'

He regarded her thoughtfully. 'I'm surprised *you* find reality so difficult to face up to,' he queried. 'You seem such a contented little soul.'

'We're not always what we seem,' she answered quickly, hiding her confusion, and was saved from further scrutiny from those searching blue eyes by the children waking up and wanting attention.

Jane went through the motions of pouring out orange squash and seeing to the more intimate needs of the youngest children with her mind still on that short, stolen interlude with Luke. It had been very sweet, but at the same time it had stretched her loyalty. She had felt at times they had reached a point of very close intimacy—not so much by what was said, but what was left unsaid. Luke had made it plain that he was attracted to her and, though this satisfied something deep inside her, it made her task of spying on him that much more distasteful.

He suggested they spent what remained of the afternoon exploring the rest of the island, and when this was explained to the children they were off without any more encouragement. For the boys, exploring meant scrambling over the rocks—for the girls, picking wild flowers.

'Is that allowed?' Jane asked. 'Picking wild flowers, I mean. There are heavy penalties for picking wild flowers on the mainland. You're not outside the law on Scilly, are you?'

'We're a very unlawful lot on Scilly,' replied Luke teasingly. 'It takes all of two policemen to keep the five islands in order.' He looked at the carpet of wild flowers that spread all around them—sea-thrift and mayweed, stonecrop and sea-campion. 'I don't think a few flowers will be missed, do you?'

Jane sighed for the days when little girls could go picking armfuls of bluebells and sit in a meadow making buttercup and daisy chains. The bulldozer and weed-killer had destroyed that innocent pastime, not little girls with their flower baskets. Later they led the children over the twin hills of Samson, stopping to explore the ruins of an old stone cottage half-way up the slope of South Hill. Luke told Jane that the last inhabitants of Samson were evacuated from the island to St Mary's in the 1850s, as life for them had fallen below subsistence level.

'Not that anybody on the Scillies had what we call a decent standard of living in those days,' he added. 'It was the daffodil industry that brought the first wave of affluence to Scilly—now, of course, it's the tourists. The tourist trade has made Scilly. I think some Scillonians feel that it might be their undoing, too—that is, if Scilly is allowed to become too commercialised.' They were standing on the top of South Hill, which was not a hill in the true sense of a word, more of a gentle slope. 'I'm not a Scillonian by birth,' he said regretfully. 'But the Scillies are my spiritual home now. I feel I belong here.'

'Where was your home?' Jane asked, forcing herself to do what Roy would call ferreting.

'I was born in Dorset, I went to school in Suffolk, I worked in London, so I didn't belong anywhere, really.' He dismissed her question with a laugh. 'I think we'd better start heading back for the beach and let the children finish what's left in the hampers, and then make for home—time's getting on.'

Jane gave out the last of the sandwiches and biscuits, and then joined him again. 'Most of the children seemed to anticipate what I want to say to them—they're very alert. Were they all born deaf?'

'Not all of them. Those with hearing-aids have a little hearing—others can lip-read. They seem to master that at an extremely young age these days, perhaps because of improved techniques in teaching. Some of them have learnt to speak, very gutturally, but at least they make themselves understood. They all sign—can you understand what they're saying?'

'They're too quick for me—but sometimes I make an inspired guess. That's something I shall have to master. What causes deafness?'

'There are many causes of deafness—a virus infection, after-effects of measles or meningitis or mumps. In those cases there's not always total deafness, and often a cure eventually. Then there are cases of congenital deafness, as, for example, an abnormality such as auditory nerve compression, or because a bone doesn't develop properly—congenital absence of the stapes, for instance. It's a wide field, and I don't know all the answers. I wish I did, but it's not my line at all.' He gave no indication of what his line had been.

'Then why did you choose to run a home for deaf children? Why not for other children—the physically or mentally handicapped, for instance? You wanted a holiday home specifically for the deaf?'

'Yes.' There was a warning note in Luke's voice that Jane ignored. Even if she had sensed his growing antipathy to being questioned, she couldn't have stopped herself—her old journalistic instincts had taken over.

'And the little girl Becky—she's a case on her own, isn't she? I mean, she doesn't attempt to make any sound at all, not like these other children. Was she born dumb, or was her dumbness caused by an illness? Is she——' Jane broke off in mid-sentence, for the man who was looking at her now was the man from the steps of the Old Bailey. 'I-I didn't mean to pry,' she stammered awkwardly. 'I was asking out of interest—to help me with my work here, I mean. I feel so—so—well—inadequate——'

His expression softened. 'Then a word of advice. The next time you question me, don't make me feel as if you're holding a gun to my head.'

She looked so crestfallen that Luke regretted his sudden brusqueness and put himself out to make amends, yet, in spite of his cheery manner, a question mark loomed in Jane's mind. Why, when she asked about Becky, did he freeze up on her? What, if anything, had he to hide?

They sailed back to St Mary's on a slack tide with a slight breeze ruffling the water. The children's energy had been sapped by a surfeit of sun and exercise, and they were too tired even to trail their hands in the water. Some had caught the sun so severely that Jane made a mental note to apply some calamine lotion to the red patches as soon as they got back to the house.

By the time she had given the children their supper and supervised bedtime, she was ready to curl up herself, but a quick, cool shower soon refreshed her, and when she was dressed again, this time in a little dress of Liberty cotton, she felt and looked good.

She joined Carole and Luke in the living-room for a pre-supper drink, and felt flattered by the look Luke gave her as he handed her a gin and tonic. He, too, had changed, and was now wearing light-coloured ducks and a navy-blue shirt. Even though he was already deeply tanned, he seemed to have caught the sun, for his forearms had darkened to the colour of copper.

Carole looked from one to the other of them. 'I needn't ask whether you've had a good time,' she said—rather archly, Jane thought. 'The picnic must have been a huge success, if empty hampers are anything to go by. Marie will be pleased—she spent all yesterday evening making those enormous pasties.'

'There were some very appetising smells coming from the kitchen as I passed,' said Luke, topping up Carole's sherry. 'By the way, where's Dinah? I haven't seen her since we got in.'

Carole gave a resigned sigh. 'She caught the bus into Hugh Town soon after lunch. I couldn't stop her; she'd finished her chores, and had taken enough notice of what I said to change into something more respectable. She said if there were any Sunday papers left, she'd bring one back for us.'

'What about her supper?'

'It's her fast day.' Carole turned to Jane. 'Dinah's idea of dieting is to stuff herself for six days, then fast on the seventh. I notice she always fasts on the day I'm doing the cooking, so I think she's trying to tell me something.'

'She's mad to miss *your* cooking,' Luke said. He rose to his feet. 'Come along, ladies, I can't wait to start on that lobster bisque.'

The soup was followed by a delicate white fish served with an oyster sauce and accompanied by duchess potatoes and mange-tout peas.

'Did you enjoy the fish?' Carole asked as Jane helped to carry the used dishes through to the kitchen afterwards.

'It was delicious—what was it? It was a new taste to me.'

'John Dory, and caught locally yesterday. It's called the fisherman's fish, because it's the fish that the fisherman chooses for his own dinner—and he should know! Now, the pudding is also special to these islands, but I didn't make it. I wish I knew how to, but I can't get hold of the recipe—it's a very closely guarded secret.' Carole took from a shelf in the pantry what looked like a chocolate slab cake. 'Chocolate fudge cake,' she said. 'Every cook uses one secret ingredient—rum or brandy or sherry—something like that. Fetch the cream, please, Jane.'

The fudge cake was all that Carole had said it was—rich and chocolatey and chewy and, served with clotted cream, made a sumptuous finish to a delightful meal. Luke had only one grumble—Cornish clotted cream wasn't what it used to be.

'I can remember a time when you could go to any dairy in Cornwall and buy clotted cream that was kept in a pottery crock, and they would send it through the post for you in a little round tin. Now it comes from a factory, already packed in plastic containers—and it isn't even the colour of cream any longer. It's white.'

'We must allow Methuselah his little grumble,' said Carole, winking at Jane.

It was one of the happiest days Jane had spent for a long time, and it was rounded off by an evening in pleasant company. She put all thoughts of Roy Barford behind her and gave herself up to the delight of the moment, and when it was finally time to go to bed she took with her the memory of Luke's warm smile as he had wished her goodnight—and she *did* have a good night, blissfully unaware of many fretful nights to come.

CHAPTER FOUR

MARIE was back. The sound of her high-pitched voice was the first thing Jane heard when she woke up the following morning. Still drowsy from sleep, she went across to the window to see what all the noise was about. In the garden below, an extremely pregnant Siamese cat was indifferently cleaning her paws, ignoring the irate woman who was screaming abuse at her over the remains of a young blackbird.

'You—you murderess!' Marie stormed. 'It isn't as if you're not fed on the very best—you don't go short of anything. No more top of the milk for you, you—you feline—I'd wring your neck if I had my way!'

Jane called down to her. 'Cats can't help their nature, Marie.'

Marie's upturned face was red with anger. 'She does it on purpose, Miss Peters, just to spite me. She's not hungry—she doesn't eat the poor things—she just pulls them to pieces and leaves them. I've watched that brood since they were eggs, in that nest over there in the honeysuckle—and this blessed cat has had every one of them. There, that's the poor father calling now. Doesn't it break your heart just to hear him?'

When Jane went down to help prepare breakfast, Marie was still venting her indignation, taking it out on the eggs she was beating. 'It's Mrs Springer's cat, she brought it back with her the last time she visited London. The first thing it did when it got here was to rip up the dining-room curtains. Perhaps you noticed the mend, Miss Peters?'

'Marie, please—can't you call me Jane? I can't remember the last time I was addressed as Miss Peters, it makes me feel like a stranger. I'm always Nurse at the hospital and Jane at home. Miss Peters sounds so stiff and starchy.'

In spite of herself, Marie smiled, but she continued her grumbling on a lower key. 'And when Mrs Springer told me what she paid for that cat I nearly passed out—it didn't seem right somehow, paying all that money for a pet. Then she paid another large sum to have it sent off to Penzance to be mated! The creature had to be mated, she demanded it—you should have heard the noise she was making. Indelicate, I thought it—thank goodness the children couldn't hear, they would have thought the thing was being tortured. Anyway, Mrs Springer says she'll get her money back when she sells the kittens—but anybody paying out good money for something that's all noise and claws and no use whatsoever needs their head examined, if you ask me!'

When Jane could get a word in, she asked what the cat was called.

'I know what *I* call her, but not in company—she's got a fancy name which I can't get my tongue round, but her common or garden name is Mitzi. You won't find her in the house now that the children are up. She hides from the children, she doesn't like them—or she's just plain jealous, more likely.'

Jane had spent an hour before going to sleep the previous evening reading the manuals Luke had given her, hoping she would have a chance to try out some of the signs she had mastered after breakfast. On the way to the playroom, which doubled up as a schoolroom for the older children, she met Carole.

'I made the acquaintance of your Mitzi this morning, but only from a distance,' Jane told her.

Carole smiled. 'Oh, you've already seen her—I'm so pleased. I meant to tell you about her yesterday, but out of sight out of mind—and poor Mitzi is mostly out of sight these days. She doesn't like strangers, and the house is always full of strangers as far as she's concerned. I suppose you noticed that she's expecting.'

Jane nodded. 'I couldn't help but notice, and I thought Siamese were renowned for being sleek.'

'Normally Mitzi is the sleekest cat you ever saw. She's beautiful, isn't she? Those voilet-blue eyes! She's a seal-point and I had her mated with a chocolate-point, so I'm interested to see who the kittens take after. Look, the children aren't ready for us yet, would you like me to show you where she's sleeping?'

Carole was in high spirits that morning, her hazel eyes sparkled and the dress she had on flattered her slim figure. Jane could not help asking herself why Carole had not remarried—she was still young and extremely attractive. Perhaps—and here thoughts of Luke loomed large—there was someone already?

There was a close relationship between sister and brother-in-law based on mutual respect and affection, or perhaps more than affection? Jane stemmed such thoughts abruptly. What was the point of conjecture when she herself would never know the outcome? As much as she hated to face up to the fact, she was only a transient visitor—one who was only staying long enough to plot mischief. She sighed so deeply, Carole heard her.

'Anything on your mind, Jane?'

To her shame, Jane found she could lie automatically by now. 'I was just wondering how I was going to cope with the children; I've hardly learnt any sign language yet.'

'Jane—Jane, give yourself a chance, you only arrived on Saturday! It took me five weeks to learn a few simple phrases. But when you do start, you'll be surprised how quickly you'll pick it up, mostly from the children themselves. Don't think of them as deaf, just think of them as children who have a different method of hearing and speaking. I nearly panicked when Luke asked me to take on the job of helping the children with their holiday tasks, but once I realised that most of the children could lip-read and were willing to make allowances for me when I couldn't understand, I soon recovered my nerve. I've fallen back on the blackboard to put over anything too difficult for me to express. Don't worry, Jane, just treat the children as you would other children, and you won't go far wrong. Don't forget they're here on holiday and are bent on enjoying themselves, so make sure they get all the fun they can.'

They had now reached the old stables at the back of which was a small brick building that had once been a wash-house. It was warm and dry in here, and tucked away in a corner was a roomy cat basket lined with a fleecy blanket. Carole looked around her.

'Mitzi's hiding somewhere—she must have seen you coming. At least I know she's taken over her new quarters—the blanket is still warm. She used to sleep in my bedroom, but I didn't want her to have her kittens there, in case the children found out about them. You know how children love kittens, they wouldn't be able to leave them alone—and that would upset Mitzi and she'd hide them goodness' knows where——' Carole broke off as a step sounded behind them. It was Luke dressed for going out—at least, he was wearing a smart jacket.

'You off to the mainland again?' Carole queried.

'No, only as far as Tresco. I've had a phone call from a one-time colleague who's holidaying over there, and he's asked me to meet him for lunch. I'll go across on one of the pleasure boats and make a day of it, as we'll have years of news to catch up on. Either of you girls want a lift into Hugh Town?'

Carole looked at Jane. 'What about you, Jane? You said something about taking some clothes to the cleaners, and

I expect you want to buy some cards and things like that. I've got some photos waiting for me at the chemist's—you could pick those up for me if you like. The island bus will bring you back, it runs every hour.'

Jane's face lit up as Carole was speaking. 'I'd love a chance to explore Hugh Town, but won't I be needed here?'

'Not if the boss says you can go,' Carole answered, grinning at Luke.

'Perhaps Jane will change her mind when she sees my old jalopy——'

'Your old jalopy!' scoffed Carole. 'You know it's the love of your life. Well, you two may have nothing better to do this morning than gadding about enjoying yourselves, but I have a group of youngsters awaiting my attention. See you later, Jane.'

'She doesn't mind me going off and leaving it all to her—she's so nice,' said Jane, thinking that nice wasn't quite the word to describe Carole, it made her sound like something to eat.'

Luke watched his sister-in-law's departure with thoughtful eyes. 'She's a good sort—she's made herself indispensable here, and I thought after London she'd find the place too quiet. She's had a raw deal from life—she lost her husband six years ago. Did she tell you?'

'Yes, but she didn't say how—was it an accident?'

'It was very sudden, but it was no accident.' A savage note sounded in Luke's voice. 'I'll tell you one day, when I've got more time, and I'll tell you about my other brother, Robin, too. They were both victims of the same illness——' Luke shrugged as if shrugging off something unpleasant. 'Come and see my old banger and tell me what you think of it.'

As Jane had already guessed, the 'old banger' Luke referred to was the sports car she had seen at the airport.

'It's a Triumph Spitfire,' said Luke proudly. 'I bought her when I was a student—she wasn't new then, and though she's quite an elderly lady now there's life in her yet. In those days there was a cult for Spitfires—there was even a Spitfire club we young rakes supported. I suppose nowadays she might be known as a collector's item—*this* collector's item, anyway.' Luke, like Carole, was in a light-hearted mood—it was as if the happy day on Samson followed by the cheerful evening the three had enjoyed together had left a legacy of contentment that they all shared.

Luke suggested he took the car round to the front of the house and waited for Jane there, as she wanted to fetch some money and her lightweight jacket. Ten minutes later, ready to go, she came lightly tripping down the steps of Nightingale House—and stopped dead at the bottom. The Spitfire was there all right, but so was Dinah, very much in possession of the passenger seat. There was no sign of Luke.

Dinah smirked. 'Going somewhere?' she said insolently.

'Yes,' answered Jane quietly. 'I'm going to Hugh Town with your uncle, and I don't think there'll be room for three of us.'

Dinah's eyes flashed with annoyance—she didn't like being reminded that Luke was her uncle. 'There's room for a little one like you in the back,' she said surlily.

The narrow seat at the back was hardly suitable for a passenger, though it made a useful space for luggage. Jane didn't know quite what to do. It would be unseemly and physically impossible to remove Dinah by force, as she was the bigger of the two, and there was no way of appealing to her in her present defiant mood. Jane was saved further embarrassment by the sudden reappearance of Luke.

He took the situation in at a glance and his face went livid. In two strides he reached the passenger door, opened it and said one word. 'Out!'

'I want to go to Hugh Town,' said Dinah at her sulkiest.

'If you're not out of this car in five seconds, I'll take you by the scruff of your neck and drag you out. I'm starting the countdown right now—five—four——'

Dinah disdained to use the door held open for her. She clambered over the steering-wheel and then over the driver's door, and, with her chin in the air, walked stiffly away, throwing Jane a look in passing that made her think that if looks could kill she would not only now be dead, but also buried.

'Sorry about that,' said Luke curtly, his good humour temporarily in short supply. 'She's going through a phase where she pushes her luck as far as it will go. She saw me bring the car round and asked if she could come to Hugh Town with me, and I told her she couldn't because I was taking you. Then I remembered some letters I wanted to post, and as soon as I went back for them she must have got in the car. Goodness knows what she was trying to prove!'

Jane thought she knew. Dinah saw Luke as a father-figure—someone to take the place of the father she had adored—and now that he had come back into her life again she wanted to show the world her proprietorial claim.

But Dinah and her wilfulness were forgotten within minutes of leaving Nightingale House. Luke had left the hood down so that they could enjoy the last of the fine weather. The wind was fresh on Jane's face—it grabbed at her hair and sent it streaming out behind her.

'Is the breeze too much for you?' asked Luke. 'I'll put the hood up if you like.'

'No—no, don't do that. I like the wind, it's exhilarating.'

Luke glanced slyly at the girl at his side. A gypsy, Dinah had referred to Jane tauntingly—and gypsy was just the word to describe her, with her long black hair and velvety eyes, and lips that were as red as the scarf she had thrown carelessly around her shoulders. Jane didn't see the admiration in Luke's eyes or the way his lips curved in a contented smile, she was too busy watching the hedgerows hurrying by. Speed was an illusion, the road wasn't built for speed—it was narrow and there were many blind corners—and as the Spitfire's finest days were over, she could only travel at a pace suited to her age.

As they approached the outskirts of Hugh Town, a bus lumbered towards them. Jane watched it go by. 'Is that the bus Carole mentioned?' she asked.

'Yes, it does a circular trip of the island and runs every hour. It starts from the park—I'll show you.'

A park! Was St Mary's big enough for a park? When Luke pointed it out to her, Jane laughed. 'You call that a park? I've seen larger gardens!'

'Don't scoff at one of St Mary's famous institutions,' Luke answered, grinning himself. 'If you only but knew. It's a very important adjunct to this town. The crowning of the Queen of the May is an annual event here when the local schoolchildren dance round the maypole, so there's room for that. All right—you may have seen bigger parks, but you won't have seen better flowers.'

Jane conceded that.

They pulled into a tiny car park with half an hour to spare. 'The pleasure boats don't leave for the off-islands until ten-fifteen,' Luke said, looking at his watch. 'Just time for a cup of coffee—what about it, Jane?'

Jane was willing; anything to prolong Luke's company. It was a ten-minute walk to the quay. Luke could have walked it in less time, but he shortened his stride to match hers. For a big man he walked lightly, like a cat, on the balls of his feet. He steered her past the coiled ropes and fishermen's nets, the lobster pots, the odd parked car, and past the bollards—some of which had once been the barrels from the old cannons up on Garrison Hill—and on to the long white building which housed the yacht club and HM

Customs, and, on its upper floor, the restaurant with views over the harbour.

'Are you hungry? They do a very nice chocolate fudge cake here,' said Luke as their coffee arrived, but regretfully Jane refused.

'I might be able to manage a slice in two or three hours' time, but not now—not after the huge helping of scrambled eggs I had for breakfast.'

Luke stirred his coffee thoughtfully. 'I hope you didn't feel I was too brusque with you yesterday on Samson, when I jumped down your throat for asking questions——'

'You didn't jump down my throat,' protested Jane, her colour rising. 'It was tactless of me, the way I fired questions about Becky like that.'

Luke gave her a long, appraising look. 'It was only natural that you wanted to find out all you could about Becky—anything to help you understand her, and I should have realised that. I thought it over afterwards, and realised how unreasonable I was. I would like to put that right now.'

Jane felt the old feeling of discomfiture coming over her. She could see Luke was on the point of confiding in her, and it gave her no satisfaction whatsoever—it only increased her guilt.

'You were interested in Becky's condition—her inability to speak. I shouldn't have shut you up, I should have explained.' Luke turned and looked out of the window, gazing into the distance with a faraway expression in his eyes. 'I expect you must have realised by now that she's someone special to me? That's the reason I'm off to Tresco to see this old friend. He and I did a spell at St Benedict's together in our younger days—he as a junior registrar and I a house-officer. We struck up quite a close friendship at the time, then we branched off on our different ways and lost touch. Scott went into psychiatry and I——' he turned and gave Jane a quizzical smile '—I think you know, or must have guessed, my speciality?'

Jane shifted uncomfortably in her chair. 'I believe you were—*are* a pathologist,' she said guardedly.

'Forensic pathologist, actually. I knew an astute young woman like you wouldn't have taken the job I offered without looking up my credentials. But that's beside the point. I haven't brought you here to talk about myself, I actually want to tell you about Becky.'

Jane felt the palms of her hands go clammy with apprehension. So this was it—this was to be her testing point—now she was going to get the information that Roy Barford would give his eye-teeth for, and, illogically, she wanted to clamp her hands over her ears and blot out anything Luke had to say.

But instead she sat immobile, steeling herself to appear impassive, and it was that inner stillness which prompted Luke into taking her more deeply into his confidence than he had intended.

He told her that Becky had a malfunction of the middle ear which was incurable, but, as for her inability to make sounds, there was no physical reason to account for that, and one ENT specialist who had examined her had suggested psychological treatment. At that time, Luke went on, Becky had been too young to be subjected to any more 'examinations'—especially as she had already suffered many upheavals in her short life.

At this point in his story, Luke hesitated, then, when he continued, he spoke as if he were weighing each word very carefully. 'She lived with foster-parents for the first couple of years of her life, and they did nothing about her deafness—perhaps her condition was not even noticed, that's not unusual. When Becky's natural father won custody of her, he did seek advice, but was told nothing could be done about her deafness. He devoted his life to her, trying to make up for her handicap—everything was subjugated to Becky. She became his vocation—his chief purpose in life—it's partly through him she can lip-read so well, and is so fluent with signing.' Again Luke lost the thread of his thoughts, and went silent, the brilliance of his eyes dulled by a touch of the melancholy Jane had noticed on two previous occasions. Surely he was referring to himself? *He* was the natural father, and if he was it answered some of the questions Roy had sent her to discover. So this was the reason an eminent forensic pathologist had thrown up an important position with the Home Office—to live abroad with his little daughter, devoting his life to her as he had just said. The pathos of the situation suddenly struck her, and it must have shown in her face, for Luke looked at her with concern.

'I hope I'm not depressing you with this tale of woe,' he said. 'But you mustn't feel depressed on Becky's account—she's a very happy child, and her handicap hasn't prevented her from enjoying a very full life. It's for my own satisfaction that I'm discussing her case with Scott Reevers, and if he wants to see Becky, which naturally he will before he can make any diagnosis, then I'll take her to Tresco to meet him; or, better still, ask him over to Nightingale House for the day.'

It was time for Luke to leave; the launches tied up to the steps at the quayside were filling up fast. The boats were double and treble-banked—in one case there were four in a line, and Luke drew Jane's attention to that. 'It's a fact of life that the boat I want is always the last one in the line,' he said with a grin. 'Which means I have the business of scrambling in and out of two or three boats to reach it—that's known as Murphy's Law. Are you coming to see me off?'

'Of course—I wouldn't miss it.'

Luke was lucky, he only had to scramble over one other boat before reaching the one going to Tresco. He was aboard and seated before he remembered the letters he had forgotten once before that morning. He took them out of his pocket and waved them at Jane. 'Would you mind posting these for me?' he shouted up at her.

Willing hands passed them along, and one of the boat's crew dashed up the steps of the quay and handed them to Jane as she stood by the handrail waiting to see the boats set off. They left at the same time like the start of a race, but once past the end of the quay they branched off in different directions—to Tresco, Bryher, St Martin's, St Agnes, the Western Rocks and the Eastern Isles, and the longest trip of all—to the Bishop Rock lighthouse.

Jane watched them until they were specks in the distance, but still she stood there a lone figure, going over in her mind what Luke had told her, remembering the pain in his voice when he had spoken of Becky. If Luke was Becky's father, who was her mother, and why had the child been farmed out to foster-parents? And, a more puzzling question still—why was Luke keeping the identity of his daughter secret? They were questions she was not likely to have answered unless—and Jane flinched at the thought—unless she went through Luke's private papers.

There was a mail-box fixed to the wall of the custom-house building, and as Jane posted Luke's letters one caught her eye, chiefly because it was an airmail. It was addressed to someone called Kirsty Brownlow, care of a box number in Victoria, Vancouver Island. There was no prefix—no Miss or Mrs—though Jane gave little thought to this at the time.

Next she went off to do her shopping, calling at the chemist's first, then to the dry-cleaners, then on to the dairy to send off cream to Miss Bruce and her brother-in-law. By this time the sky was leaden-colour, so Jane decided to cut short her shopping trip and return to Nightingale House. She caught the bus with minutes to spare, and, though it was less than a twenty-minute drive to her destination, it was raining quite heavily when she alighted. She sprinted the last few hundred yards to the house, and arrived breathless, with her hair hanging in damp streamers.

As soon as she stepped over the threshold she became aware of an aura of tension, as if the old house was holding its breath with apprehension. She hurried to her room, changed into dry clothes and gave her hair a brisk towelling, and it was while she was doing this that she noticed the top drawer of her dressing-table was slightly open. She knew she had left it closed. She put down the towel and went across to see if anything was wrong, and realised immediately that someone had been going through her things.

Each drawer had been thoroughly gone over, though nothing was missing. Jane knew she was in no position to feel resentful, considering that she was planning to do something similar to Luke, but the knowledge that someone had been searching through her private possessions, and feeling the outrage it engendered, made her feel unclean—not because of what had been done to her, but because of what she was contemplating doing to Luke.

She made her way down to the kitchen, turning over in her mind whether to mention it or not. Perhaps the culprit was one of the children, in which case Carole should be told, but Jane felt uneasy about doing so. Marie was busy putting the finishing touches to lunch, and as Jane went to the dresser-drawer to get out the tablecloth Marie looked up and mouthed the one word—'trouble'.

Before Jane could ask her what she meant by that, Carole came into the room, and clearly there had been another upset between mother and daughter. 'Jane, just a minute,' said Carole, and her voice was barely steady.

'Trouble,' Carole said when they were out in the hall, only, unlike Marie, she said it aloud and she said it bitterly.

'You mean with Dinah?' Jane asked sympathetically.

Tears welled in Carole's eyes. 'I'm going to make a fool of myself any minute. Come up to my room and I'll tell you all about it.' She led the way to the stairs.

'What about the children—is it all right to leave them?' Jane asked.

'They'll be all right. They're all in the playroom because of the rain, and I've set them some puzzles to keep them amused. In any case, Marie will be serving their lunch soon. This way, Jane, the room at the end.'

Carole's room was similar in lay-out to Jane's, only larger, and had those little personal touches that the guest-room lacked. She pulled out a small easy chair for Jane, but was too restless to sit herself, and paced about the strip of floor between the bed and the window instead.

'I didn't know until after you and Luke had left that Dinah had tried to gatecrash your outing this morning,' she said. 'She came flouncing into the house in one of her bad tempers, and took her disappointment out on me. I'm afraid I lost my temper in return, and told her in no uncertain terms what I thought of her and her tantrums. That sort of thing goes on between us all the time lately,' Carole added wearily. 'Anyway, when I went upstairs later to change my tights, I found that someone had been searching through my dressing-table drawers—Dinah, of course, who else? Yes, you may well look like that, Jane—I expect you're asking yourself why. I'll tell you—that little vixen had cut the straps off every one of my under slips! I felt sick when I saw what she'd done.'

It was at this point that Jane began to feel a little sick herself, but Carole, in the full flow of her agitation, gave her no chance to interrupt. 'I accept that Dinah is unruly and rebellious, and defiant to the point of driving me crazy,' she went on, husky with tears, 'but I've never known her to be vicious or to behave spitefully. I can stomach anything but malice, and I don't mind telling you, I went beserk when I saw what she had done. I just grabbed my underçlothes and went looking for her, and found her in the morning-room listening to that stupid little radio she carries around with her everywhere.

'I didn't say a word—I just stood there and held up my slips, and do you know what her reaction was? She laughed—*she laughed*! I lost all control then, and slapped her face—I've never raised a finger to her before, and that stopped her laughing quickly enough! She gave me a horrified look. I felt just as horrified; I could see the marks of my fingers right across her cheek. Then she ran out of the room, and I haven't seen her since, and that must be two hours ago now. Oh, Jane, what am I to do about her? I'm at my wits' end!'

Carole was looking away, otherwise she would have seen the anguish that flickered in and out of Jane's eyes. 'You're so positive it was Dinah who cut the straps from your underclothes?' she asked unsteadily.

Carole was emphatic about that. 'Of course it was Dinah—who else could it have been? She did it to get her own back on me for the telling-off I gave her. Goodness knows I don't care a fig about my undies—that's something that can easily be put right—it's the malice behind her actions that got under my skin. There's something evil about malice, and whatever else Dinah is, I don't want to believe that she's evil.' Carole's legs gave way, and she flopped on the bed, covering her face with her hands.

Jane swallowed. 'Carole, I have something to confess to you,' she said.

There was such urgency in Jane's voice that Carole looked up immediately. She listened without interruption and, at Jane's explanation of Becky's obsession with tying like toys to like and how Jane had shown her how to use shoulder-straps in lieu of string, a bewilderment of expressions crossed her face. Jane expected a blast of indignation to follow the conclusion of her story, but instead she found herself being hugged and kissed instead.

'What a blessed relief—what a relief!' Carole didn't know whether to laugh or cry. 'Oh, my poor Dinah, she must have thought I'd finally flipped! I must go and find her; she'll be in Hugh Town, I expect—I'll take the minibus and go in search of her. Oh, it's such a weight off my mind to know she didn't deliberately cut into my undies. How I've wronged her, and I do love her so, though I'm not very good at showing it. Now I suppose I'd better go and make my peace with her—I'll grovel if I have to——'

'You don't have to grovel—just tell Dinah what you've just told me, that you love her.'

'Oh, Jane, if it were only as easy as that, but I'll try.' Carole looked at herself in the glass and grimaced. 'I look about ninety—now, where did I put my bag? A dab of blusher hides a multitude of sins.' Deftly she repaired the ravages of the past few hours.

'Aren't you just the tiniest bit angry with me or with Becky for what's happened?' Jane asked warily.

Carole smiled at her through the mirror. 'Bless you, Jane, I couldn't be angry with you if I tried—you acted in all good faith, and how could I be angry with little Becky? She didn't know that what she was doing was wrong. Poor little kiddie. Wish me luck,' she said as she went off in a swirl of skirts. She stopped at the door and looked back—the picture of a happy woman. 'If you want to do me a favour, wheedle my shoulder-straps away from Becky and sew them back on for me. Bye for now.'

Jane found Becky in her own little bedroom, a one-time dressing-room that led from one of the dormitories. She was sitting on the floor with the cut-off shoulder-straps in a neat pile by her side, and all around her an odd assortment of stuffed animals which she was attempting to tie together in the manner Jane had shown her. It took a lot of patience on Jane's part, and a good deal of guessing on Becky's, before the child gradually realised that she had no right to the pretty ribbons, and it was with a very downcast expression that she reluctantly handed back her spoils. Seeing that tears weren't far away, Jane vowed to herself that never again she would act irresponsibly in front of a child—not now that she had been taught the hard way how good intentions could sometimes come to grief.

Carole and Dinah didn't return until after lunch, Carole looking pale and jaded. She whispered to Jane in passing, 'It's back to square one, but that's better than open warfare.' Dinah rushed straight to her room, her eyes red and swollen with crying, and Jane felt a rush of compassion for her. Perhaps Dinah wasn't the hardbitten little rebel she tried to make out, but just another misunderstood teenager.

Marie, like the good-hearted soul she was, had marshalled the children together—Becky, too—and taken them for an afternoon walk. The rain had stopped and they were well wrapped up against the chilling mist that shrouded the island. Sea and sky had merged into one, making a swirling grey curtain that obscured all sight of the other islands, and every ten seconds the foghorn from Round Rock lighthouse sounded a warning boom.

It was now three o'clock; the chimes from the grandfather clock in the hall echoed through the quiet house. Jane could no longer avoid the harsh fact that she was here for a purpose, and what better opportunity to achieve that purpose than now when she virtually had the house to herself, as both Carole and Dinah were sleeping off the after-effects of their quarrel.

She remembered that Luke had told her during their drive to St Mary's that morning that he had written out some letters in rough, and asked her to type them out for him if she found the opportunity. There was a portable

typewriter on the knee-hole desk in his study, and there was
another desk, too, Jane had noticed when she had been in that
room before—a large roll-top desk. It had taken her eye
because her father had owned a similar one.

In either of the desks she might be lucky enough to find
some small piece of evidence that could forestall Roy Barford
for the present. She had no intention of passing on what Luke
had told her in confidence that morning, or her conviction that
he was Becky's father. What she wanted was some small thing
that would satisfy Roy without incriminating Luke—though
she knew, even as the thought came to her, that was a
contradiction in terms. Roy would not be satisfied with
anything that did not incriminate Luke.

Planning in one's mind to go through someone else's
private papers was quite a different matter from actually
putting that plan into execution, as Jane found when
confronted by the task. The knee-hole desk held nothing
more suspicious than ledgers, writing paper and typing
paper. She took out a sheet of writing paper and inserted it
into the typewriter so that if she should hear anyone
coming, Carole for instance, she could act as if she were
about to type. For the same reason she left the door slightly
open, to make it easier to hear someone coming.

She walked across to the other desk that was placed just
under the window. The mist had thickened, deadening all
sounds—it was the first time she had not heard the
songbirds since arriving at Nightingale House. She thought
of Marie out there somewhere with the children, and hoped
she would bring them home soon, but all these thoughts
were only to put off that which she dreaded—to start
searching this desk.

Her last hope that she would find the desk locked wasn't
to be—the top went up easily, the little slats disappeared
into the slot made for them. Luke was a tidy man—there
wasn't a paper out of place, and each of the pigeon-holes

was filled with neat stacks of letters, notebooks and diaries.
I can't do it, she thought. I just can't go through anybody's
private papers. Then, unbidden, an image of Jamie floated
before her eyes. Wasn't he worth burying her conscience
for? A conscience she could always bring out and dust down
once this hateful task was over. She didn't hesitate any
longer—feverishly she began to rifle through the contents of
the desk, and almost at once she came across a photograph
of a young and attractive girl in a bikini.

With her heart racing from a strange mix of
disappointment and shame, she studied the photo carefully.
Instinctively, she felt that this girl was Becky's mother; she
could see a similarity in the set of the head and the narrow,
pointed face. The girl was smiling into the camera, and
behind her a man lazed on the sands, his head half-turned,
but recognisable as Luke when several years younger. Jane
turned the photo over and read the words on the
back—'Kirsty—Bondi Beach—Sydney'.

Engrossed as she was, she was unaware that someone had
quietly entered the room and was watching her—unaware,
that was, until she felt the hairs rise on the back of her neck
and a sense of apprehension, like shock waves, sweep over
her. Then, slowly, she lifted her head and faced the
unsmiling man in the doorway.

CHAPTER FIVE

NEVER had Luke's eyes looked so brilliant as they did at that moment. They registered shock, outrage and disappointment in turn. Jane felt her legs turn to water, and her heart fluttered in her throat like a frightened bird.

In two strides he had crossed the room, and when he reached her he snatched the photograph from her hand. 'Is *this* what you were looking for?' he asked quietly.

Jane was not deceived by the quietness of his manner, she could sense the undercurrent of puzzlement and uneasiness in his voice. She knew there was no further point in carrying on her deception, but even so she started to babble out excuses.

'I was looking for an address book. I—I couldn't quite make out the address on one of the letters you left me to type out . . .' Her voice faltered and trailed off, and when Luke didn't answer, she floundered even more. 'I hoped to get all the letters finished before you returned. I—I didn't expect you back so soon——'

'That's obvious,' was the curt rejoinder. Luke looked across at the typewriter and the sheet of pristine writing paper in the carriage. 'My address book is in the top drawer of the knee-hole desk, as you must have seen when you looked for the paper. And——' indicating the photo '—this doesn't look much like an address book to me!' His sarcasm was searing.

'I—I thought—I mean, didn't——'

'Stop it!' His disappointment in her was quickly giving way to anger. 'If you can't lie with conviction, don't lie

76

at all.' Luke felt sick at heart and made no effort to hide it. He would have sworn an oath that Jane was completely trustworthy. He could not believe that anybody with her air of sincerity could stoop to lie and cheat, and that was how he felt—cheated. He had been taken in by this brown-eyed girl with her soft voice and winning ways, and it was that feeling of betrayal that sparked off his anger.

He waved the photo in her face. 'Is this what you were looking for—presuming you were looking for something specific—or were you just rifling through my things out of idle curiosity?'

Jane had no idea of the pathos behind that question, of Luke's hope that her actions had been prompted by nothing worse than curiosity—a despicable failing, but pardonable. The alternative was hard for him to accept, for what sinister motive had prompted Jane to pry into his personal effects? And why should this girl who had only come into his life two days ago do this to him? What did she want of him—this girl with a mixture of guilt and despair in her wide, dark eyes?

A hidden memory flickered in and out of Luke's mind, and he took Jane's chin and held her face to the light.

'Where have I seen you before?' he demanded. 'Somewhere—I know I have. Come on, tell me!' As his control snapped he began to shake her, and only stopped when he saw her flinch. He dropped his hands to his side and stood there frowning at her, breathing hard like a man who had been running, then he walked to the door, locked it and pocketed the key.

'You don't leave here until I've got to the bottom of this matter,' he said grimly, 'and for a start you can tell me where I've seen you before.'

I can't fight him, Jane thought. I can't even fight myself any more. Once before she had stood like this, facing this angry man—staring with a sense of helplessness into a pair of furious blue eyes. The years fell away and she was nineteen again, and at that time a cub reporter on Roy's paper, the *Moonraker—Muckraker* to its rivals—and had been sent to the Old Bailey to cover a murder trial.

Luke had been a Home Office pathologist who had been called as an expert witness, and from the first day—for the wide-eyed girl in the Press box, anyway—he had dominated the proceedings.

Jane's job had not been to report on the trial, which had been that of an open-and-shut case—she was to single out the wife of the man in the dock, and to try and find out more about his personal life. What had driven a quiet, respectable man to turn to violence, for instance?

'The wife'll talk—they all talk when a cheque-book is waved under their noses,' Roy had leered. 'Just get the bare bones of the chap's life story. We can pad it out here—something to tickle our readers' fancy, you know the sort of thing!'

But Jane hadn't got her story—not that she had tried very hard, having suddenly realised that she hadn't got the stomach for that kind of journalism. Anyway, the wife had refused to talk and had scorned a bribe—much to Jane's relief. Now she had a valid excuse to take back to Roy Barford.

She had been standing on the steps of the Old Bailey watching the grief-stricken woman being led away by a relative when she in her turn had been accosted by the tall, broad-shouldered figure of Lucian Springer. The look he had given her from those intense blue eyes was to remain with her for years to come.

'That was a lesson for you in dignity and integrity,' he'd said, his voice charged with scorn. 'I overheard the sordid bargain you were trying to strike with poor Mrs Coombe, and I admire her for the way she stood up to you. What kind of person are you, working for a tatty little rag like the *Moonraker*? Can't you get yourself a decent job, a job you can be proud of? You look intelligent enough.' Then his voice had softened; he had even managed a faint sardonic smile. 'Go back and tell your editor to find someone more like himself—heartless and without scruples. You're obviously in the wrong job.'

Yes, she had known she was in the wrong job, and a year later she had left to start training as a nurse—but now her past had caught up with her, and she had no option but to confess everything to this hard-faced man.

Hard-faced Luke certainly was at that moment, but it was not a hardness reflected in his heart. A faint pity stirred him as he stared down at the wan-faced girl, and, much against his better judgement, he felt an overwhelming desire to take her in his arms and kiss away the sadness that showed in her eyes and the droop of her mouth. But because he resented such weakness, he overcame it in a show of aggression.

'I can see it's going to take a long time to get to the bottom of this affair, so you had better sit down.'

Jane straightened her shoulders. 'I'm quite all right,' she said, showing the first trace of defiance since Luke had surprised her.

In no mood to argue, he took her forcibly by the elbow, walked her across to a sofa and sat her down. He didn't sit himself, but towered over her. 'Now answer my question—where have we met before?'

'Outside the Old Bailey.'

'I didn't hear that—say it again, louder!'

'On the steps of the Old Bailey.'

The Old Bailey? His mind raced. 'When?'

'Five years ago.'

Five years ago, Luke repeated to himself—*that* year—the year after Ned died, the year he first heard about Robin. He took a deep breath, steadying himself, reached for a chair, and sat down rather heavily. For a moment or two he forgot the girl sitting opposite, he was lost in his memories of the year that still haunted him. Then his mouth hardened into a grim line as he finally recalled her, plucking her from a kaleidoscope of lost images. She had looked so demure in her neat little navy and blue outfit, like a schoolgirl in her Sunday best, standing in the shadow of that grim fortress, staring up at him with a startled expression.

Yes, he remembered. He had overheard her badgering some poor woman whose husband had just been sent down for fifteen years. He had told her just what he had thought of her, and she hadn't said a word in her own defence, just stared at him with those liquid brown eyes—just as she was staring at him now.

'I remember,' he said. 'I remember that case very well, but what has that to do with you now rifling my desk—or with this photo?' As he spoke he flicked the photograph of the girl in the bikini with his finger.

'I wasn't looking for that photo—I wasn't looking for any photos,' said Jane wretchedly. 'I was looking for something that would incriminate you—a diary or letters of something like that.' She twisted her hands together, not knowing how to go on. 'The editor I used to work for offered me money to write one more news story for him. He wanted me to dig up something about your past—to find out why four years ago you gave up your position at the Home Office and went abroad, and why you returned to England last year and subsequently opened a home for deaf children in the Scilly Isles.'

Jane spoke the words without any expression in her voice, as if repeating a lesson well learnt. Her sense of relief was enormous—it was out now, no more secrets, nothing more to hide. All she had to do now was to wait for the vituperation she felt was coming. But Luke sat silent, his eyes two narrow slits in a face like stone.

'And how much am I worth—I mean, how much are you

being paid for this sensational story?' he drawled at length.

Jane swallowed, her mouth was so dry she could hardly speak. 'I don't rightly know yet—but—but it will be in the region of several thousand pounds,' she whispered.

Luke rose to his feet in such a fury that his chair went flying. He picked it up again, and that simple action seemed to calm him, for he smiled at Jane in an ugly way. 'Several thousands, eh? Not bad payment for a holiday job. And how do you propose to spend it?'

Tears welled in Jane's eyes, and she put the back of her hand against her mouth as if to stop herself crying out. 'I can't go on like this,' she said brokenly. 'Please have a heart and let me go—I've told you the truth——'

'But not the whole truth,' he retorted. 'Come along, now, play fair—if you're going to make money out of me, I have a right to know how it's going to be spent.'

'If I tell you, will you promise to keep it to yourself?' she pleaded. 'Treat it as something told to you in confidence——'

He gave a short, unhumorous bark of laughter. 'That's rich, coming from you! I'll make no promises to you, my girl—so, whatever you have to say, you'd better say quickly before my patience runs out.'

Jane clasped and unclasped her hands in agitation. 'I—I told you about the car accident in which my sister and her husband were involved——' She spoke so softly that again Luke interrupted to tell her to speak up. She raised her voice a little, but it was still husky and indistinct. 'My nephew Jamie was with them; he was asleep on the back seat. They were driving overnight from Devon to our house is Esher to see my father before it was too late. He'd been ill for weeks, and then he took a sudden turn for the worse. It was a foggy night, and their car was involved in a pile-up on the motorway. Sue and Jim escaped injury, but—but,' Jane took a deep breath, 'the back of the car took the full impact, and little Jamie was badly hurt. A splinter of metal pierced his brain, and he was on a life-support machine for several weeks. When he recovered——' Jane hesitated, then blurted on '—but he's never recovered—that's just it. He's like a baby, worse than a baby—he can't speak or move or understand. He doesn't recognise anybody—he's—he's just a vegetable——'

The breakdown Jane had been fighting against overcame her at this point, and she began to cry. Luke watched her for a minute or two in silence, with the face of, a tortured man, then he went across to the drinks cupboard and poured her a brandy.

'Drink this,' he said, and when she tried to push the glass away, he snapped at her. 'Drink this and don't argue. It will make you feel better.'

Jane took a quick gulp. It didn't ease the dryness of her mouth, but it was like fire in her veins, warming her. Colour came back to her face.

'And what has this shocking story got to do with you coming here under false pretences? We come back to that every time, don't we?' Luke sounded weary.

Jane took another large mouthful of brandy. Whether it was the effect of the spirit or because Luke now seemed more amenable, she found she had lost her fear of him. It was even becoming a relief to unburden herself—to tell him everything. Roy's image appeared momentarily before her inner eye, but she shut her mind to him. Let him do his worst—it didn't matter any longer.

The chimes of the clock in the hall rang through the house, and Luke stirred. He had been staring out of the window into the mist that was growing thicker by the minute, now he turned and came back to Jane, to question her further, his manner no longer aggressive. He seemed rather restrained.

'Tell me the connection between your little nephew and

me,' he said. 'Then I'll let you go.'

Jane would have told him without that promise. Now she could talk freely. 'Susan and Jim sold up their farm in Devon after my father died and moved in with me. The farm hadn't paid—it had been a pipe-dream on Jim's part—he was tired of an office routine. Father had left the family house to Susan and me, so we shared it, and Esher was near enough to the hospital for them to visit Jamie daily. They couldn't accept that Jamie's condition would never improve. They went to one brain surgeon after another, but they were always told the same thing—that an operation to remove the splinter was out of the question. For one thing, the odds on Jamie dying on the operating-table were too great, and, secondly, if he did survive the operation, there would be no guarantee that there would be any improvement in his condition—he might even become worse. There was only one person in the world they were told who would risk doing such an operation, and that was Erik Tollesbury.'

'Ah, yes,' Luke looked thoughtful. 'I've heard great things of that clinic of his in Los Angeles. Tollesbury can afford to take risks because his fees are so high. Did your sister and brother-in-law consider approaching him?'

'No—no,' said Jane quickly. 'They hadn't got that sort of money. We did talk it over, of course, and I suggested raising a loan on the house, but Jim wouldn't hear of it. He said it wasn't fair to me, and also, thinking of the future, if ever the house was sold, Susan's half would go towards—well, a fund for Jamie, should—should anything happen to them, and he still needed care. Then out of the blue I had a phone call from my old boss.' She drained her glass and looked around for somewhere to put it. Luke took it from her. 'I hadn't heard from him since I left the *Moonraker*, but he knew all about Jamie—he'd read an account of the accident in the paper and he made other enquiries. He knows how and where to find out about things.'

'No doubt,' Luke put in drily. 'Don't tell me this man offered to pay to send your nephew to the Tollesbury Clinic? Is he a philanthropist, or did he get up a fund or something like that?'

Jane held Luke's gaze, staring back at him unflinchingly. 'It was his payment for my article on you.'

Luke's eyes narrowed. 'I get it now—sort of emotional blackmail. And, of course, you agreed.'

It hadn't been as simple as that.

Some weeks previously, Jane had faced Roy Barford across the desk in his dingy office. 'Remember that man?' he had said, flicking a photograph of Luke across to her. Of course Jane had remembered—she had never forgotten him, and he had changed little in five years. 'I've got an old score to settle with him,' Roy had gone on. 'Nothing you know about, ducky. It happened after your time.' Then he had put his proposition to her—she was to find out all she could about Luke Springer's past. Why had he left the Home Office? Why had he gone abroad? Why was he now living in the Scillies in charge of a holiday home for deaf children? If Jane could come up with those answers and write it up into a story for his paper, he would pay the bill for Jamie's operation at the Tollesbury Clinic.

'Why me?' Jane had cried in a wild fashion, feeling that a trap was about to be sprung on her. 'You employ better journalists than I ever was—you were always criticising my work.'

'You've got two things in your favour, ducky. You're a nurse, and Springer is advertising for a nurse; here, read for yourself—that's your lever to get entry into his household. More importantly still—you've got the incentive! A cure for young Jamie in exchange for your story about Springer—not much to ask, is it?'

It hadn't seemed much at the time. It wasn't until it had been too late, and Jamie and Susan were already on their way to California, that Jane had realised the full extent of the deception that was involved.

'Why can't I just go to Dr Springer and ask for his story?' she had asked, a question that had aroused Roy's fury.

'You little fool—this is to be an undercover job. Luke Springer wouldn't let you past the door if he suspected you had any connections with the *Moonraker*. It's a stroke of luck that he's advertising for a nurse; I spotted the opportunity at once. Believe me, ducky, Luke Springer isn't going to talk to anybody about his past—that's what makes me so sure he must have something to hide.' And Roy had then lit a cigar with the air of someone whose plans were all working out to his satisfaction.

Jane's last hope then had been that she wouldn't get the job—but fate had decreed otherwise, and now she sat in Luke's study, staring miserably at her hands.

'So you had to make a choice between your nephew's welfare or mine?' Luke asked evenly.

'Yes.' No more excuses; she was too tired.

'If you had to make the same choice over again, now that you've seen the set-up here, knowing that your decision could affect those very near and dear to me—would your answer be the same?'

Jane hesitated only long enough to think of Jamie as he was now, and how he could be again—the lovable, loving, intelligent little boy he once was. 'Yes,' she said quietly.

Luke looked defeated. 'Well, that was honest, anyway.' He hesitated then asked, 'The question is—where do we go from here?'

Jane rose unsteadily to her feet. 'I think I'd better go and pack. The sooner I leave the better for all of us.'

Luke laughed—not a pleasant sound. 'In this?' he said, rapping the window-pane. 'There'll be no getting off this island today. All flights will be grounded, and if it gets any thicker I doubt whether the *Scillonian* will be able to sail. You'll have to stay until the mist clears.' His voice registered neither regret nor approval. He seemed not to care one way or the other.

Jane felt trapped. She couldn't stay another minute now that Luke knew everything about her. What if he told Carole—and Marie, too? She couldn't face them—she hadn't got the moral courage to face them if they knew. She began to panic.

Luke unlocked the door. 'You're free to go. And don't worry, I'll keep your guilty secret,' he said, as if he could read her thoughts. He gave her a long, steady look. 'I can understand your motives now, but I can't condone them—I think you went to unnecessary lengths to deceive me. I still don't feel too sure in my mind about you; I still can't make up my mind whether you've been completely open with me or not. I'll need a few days to think things over, and then we'll have another talk. Until then, we'll carry on as usual.'

He held the door open for her, and Jane walked through and along the corridor to her own room. She was trembling so much when she got there that when she filled a glass with water and put it to her lips it splashed down the front of her jumper.

She sat on the edge of her bed, rocking herself to and fro in silent misery, too keyed up even to find relief in tears. The brief, happy period of kinship with Luke was over—the relationship that had held such promise was doomed. All she could do now was to get through her last few days at Nightingale House as unobtrusively as possible, and try to put out of her mind forever the man who had become so dear to her.

Jane skipped tea that afternoon. The children were back—she could hear the noise of their excitement and the sound of their feet drumming on the stairs. Nobody came to enquire after her. She lay on her bed trying to rest, but getting little respite from her thoughts. Finally, when it was time to go down and prepare the children for supper, she dragged herself into the bathroom and splashed her face all over with cold water. It refreshed her, but couldn't wash away her lethargy. Her reflection stared back at her—it looked awful. Her eyes were like bottomless pits, and her face ashen-coloured beneath its tan. Her hair was in a mess, too, where she had tossed and turned on the bed. She brushed it out and braided it, then piled it on top of her head. Usually she had no need of blusher, but now she applied it liberally, and also reddened her lips. She changed into a black accordion-pleated skirt and a scarlet sleeveless top. Just because she felt down and out, there was no need to look like it, too.

Carole, when she met her at the top of the stairs, looked her up and down and gave an imitation of a wolf-whistle.

'And where are you off to, my pretty maid?'

'To bath the children.'

Carole laughed. 'In that get-up? You'd better borrow one of Marie's overalls.' She peered closer into Jane's face and her smile went. 'You look very peaky, Jane. Anything the matter?'

'Just a bit of a head; I tried to sleep it off.'

'I guessed you were lying down, that's why I didn't disturb you. I had a lovely sleep.' They had reached the foot of the stairs. 'Did Luke tell you about our guest?'

'Guest?'

'Well, kind of guest. You know Luke went over to Tresco to meet his old friend Scott Reevers? Dr Reevers decided to come back to St Mary's with him, as he'd promised himself a few days on this island. As soon as they saw the mist rolling up, they decided to get over to St Mary's while there was still time. Dr Reevers has booked into a hotel in Hugh

Town, and Luke is dining with him tonight—he's going to invite him over tomorrow. You've just missed Luke. He didn't take the car—he's walking into town.'

Jane heard this news with a sense of reprieve—she had dreaded facing Luke at supper. As it was, supper turned out to be *dîner à deux* that evening, as Dinah had gone to bed—rather, she hadn't got up from the afternoon—saying she didn't feel well, and Marie preferred to have her supper in the kitchen watching television.

'Is there anything wrong with Dinah?' asked Jane as she toyed with her chicken casserole.

'Just the usual—sulking. She's going to make me suffer for misjudging her; she won't let me forget that in a hurry, and will use it as a weapon against me at every opportunity, but I don't mind, as long as it clears the air between us. I feel like a pick-me-up tonight, and you look as if you could do with one. Join me in a bottle of claret, Jane?'

'No, I couldn't really,' Jane protested, feeling she had no right to Luke's best claret, but Carole wouldn't take no for an answer and poured her out a generous glassful. 'We'll leave the rest of the bottle for Luke,' she said. 'He'll want something to warm him when he gets in.'

After supper Carole joined Marie in the kitchen. There was a film on television starring Paul Newman she wanted to watch. Jane went up to her room to write a letter to Roy Barford. It wasn't a lengthy letter; she stated quite simply that she couldn't go on with the deception, and was leaving St Mary's on the first available flight. Any expenses he had already incurred on Jamie's account she would refund, and she would also be responsible for the fees due to the Tollesbury Clinic.

How she would raise the money when the time came, she wasn't sure—vague thoughts of raising a loan from a bank crossed her mind. She would have to keep it secret from Sue and Jim, for they would never agree. Susan would present no problems—she had clutched at the chance of taking Jamie to the Tollesbury Clinic as a drowning man clutched at a straw, and had accepted without question Jane's story that her old paper was putting up the money in exchange for Jamie's story. It was the sort of thing that had been done before. It wouldn't be so easy to pull the wool over Jim's eyes, but as he, too, was only too ready to accept any help available, he wouldn't enquire too deeply into ways and means. Jane signed her letter and sealed it, and, putting on an anorak with a hood attached, went out to post it—anxious to send it on its way as quickly as possible.

The clock in the hall was striking nine o'clock as she let herself out of the door, and almost at once she found herself in a different world. A world where the last of the daylight was obscured by a thick, moist blanket of mist. It was uncannily quiet, and there was no movement of any kind—only the drip, drip, drip as the mist evaporated and fell like raindrops from the trees.

She had seen a letter-box at the top of the lane, one of those small boxes attached to a post—there were no other kind on Scilly. She had remembered it because she had smiled at the wording on the plate that gave the times of collection. There were no stated times, it just said, 'Collections depend on sailing times.' She didn't smile now—she just wished for some magic formula to get her message to Roy without delay. Anything to stop him phoning her again. And that put the idea into her mind—there was a phone box near the letter-box. She could still post her letter, then phone Roy and tell him there was some news on the way to him.

She put the call through to Roy's home address, reversing the charges as she had no money on her, and he answered almost immediately. She could picture him, lolling in an easy chair, a whisky and soda on a nearby table, the inevitable cigar between his fingers, and, of course, the phone always at the ready.

As soon as he heard her voice, he barked, 'And about time, too! Any news?'

'Yes, but I won't stop to tell you now, as this is an expensive call. I've just posted a letter off to you explaining——'

'Hang the expense, ducky. What's the news?'

Jane took the plunge. 'Roy, I can't go on with it—I'm coming home.'

There was such a long pause, she felt he had hung up on her. 'Roy?'

Roy's voice came silkily over the phone. 'Ducky, there's no way you're going to walk out on me now. I just won't let you—I've staked too much on this——'

'I'll repay you every penny——'

'I'm not talking about money—I'm talking about good old healthy revenge. I'm out to get Springer and I will, and you're going to help me—you owe me something, ducky. Remember how you walked out on me once before? I don't forget things like that——'

Jane hung up on him. She suddenly felt so faint, she had to cling to the door for support. Roy was deranged—no man in his right senses would make threats like that. Revenge? What had Luke ever done to him that made Roy hate him so? Jane doubted whether Luke had ever heard Roy's name. She had not mentioned it in their exchange earlier—and the *Moonraker* was not a paper Luke would read.

She pulled her hood back over her head and went out once more into the mist. It seemed thicker now that the last of the daylight had gone. She felt her way carefully with her feet, having nothing to guide her, only knowing she had reached the lane by the sound of dripping trees.

Suddenly she became aware of another sound—footsteps—someone was walking just behind her. Her heart jumped into her mouth, suffocating her with a sudden,

irrational fear. Irrational, because she knew she was on
Scilly and not in one of the back streets near St Benedict's
where it wasn't safe to be out after dark.

Instinctively she quickened her step, relieved out of all
proportion when the gates of Nightingale House loomed
out of the mist. Now she would lose her follower, but the
footsteps followed her up the drive, and that could mean
only one thing—the footsteps belonged to Luke. She waited
for him; she couldn't do otherwise. 'I didn't know it was
you behind me,' she said.

'Really? I thought you were trying to get away from me,
the way you put on speed,' he said drily. 'I saw you come
out of the phone box—it's well lit up just there. I presume
our phone is out of order?'

He knew it wasn't, he was just testing her, Jane thought.
He was never going to trust her again, she knew that.

'I went to post a letter—then on the spur of the moment,
decided to make a phone call. There was nothing
underhand about it,' she said dully.

'A phone call that couldn't wait, presumably?'

'I was calling the editor of the *Moonraker* at his home
address to tell him that the deal I made with him is off.
That I'm leaving St Mary's as soon as I can.'

'Ah. Then that wasn't a wasted call.' But there was a
certain inflection about Luke's voice that sounded like
disappointment . . .

CHAPTER SIX

'LUKE! You're back. Oh, thank goodness! Oh, Luke . . .' As they emerged into the hall, Carole appeared at the top of the stairs and came flying down to them.

Luke caught her by her shoulders and steadied her. 'Carole! For goodness' sake, what's happened?'

'It's Dinah. I went up to her a moment ago to see how she was—and Luke, she's running a fever. Her throat's so sore she can hardly speak—she's ill, Luke. She's gravely ill. And she was as right as rain this afternoon—wasn't she?' Carole appealed to Jane, but, without waiting for her answer, turned wildly to Luke again.

'It's Ned all over again. This is how Ned went—healthy one moment and then—then . . .' Carole buried her head in Luke's shoulder and her words came muffled. 'Oh, Luke, I was so vile to her this morning. I said such rotten things—and now she may—she's . . .'

Luke gave his sister-in-law a gentle shake. 'Take hold of yourself, Carole, you're becoming hysterical. I don't suppose Dinah has anything worse than a severe cold, but I'll go up and check. You stay here with Jane.' And Luke shot off, taking the stairs two at a time, and his urgency, instead of reassuring Carole, only added to her fears.

She stared bleakly at Jane. 'I expect you think I'm making a fuss about nothing. But this is just how it happened to Ned. No warning—a sudden chill, a fever—and then—and then——' She made a tremendous effort to pull herself together.

'He died of a rare form of anaemia—the very last illness

I would have associated with Ned, as he always looked so fit. He was fit right up to the end—and then it all happened so suddenly. Luke told me it was acute aplastic anaemia—Ned died before he could be given the transfusion of white blood cells that might have saved him. Two years later his brother Robin died of the same disease, though he had it in the chronic form—he'd suffered from it for years without telling us. I panicked then—I thought it must be a familial thing, though Luke assured me it wasn't. I wasn't convinced—I thought Luke was holding something back. I still do. Jane, can you imagine what I go through every time Dinah feels sick—always with the thought of Ned at the back of my mind? But this time, what with the high fever and complaining about a pain in her side——' She broke off as Luke came swiftly down the stairs, and ran to him.

Luke was reassuring. 'Dinah has *not* got aplastic amaemia,' he said firmly. 'She's ill, poor kid—I'm not denying that. She's got all the classic symptoms of glandular fever—enlarged lymph nodes in her neck, a sore throat, enlarged spleen—but there's no need to be worried. Glandular fever is unpleasant, but it's not fatal. Dinah is going to feel very groggy for the next two weeks, then she'll slowly improve, but don't expect her to be really a hundred per cent until the autumn. She'll go through months of general debility first.'

'What kind of a mother am I not to have seen this coming on?' Carole cried.

'What kind of a doctor am I not to have spotted the symptoms? That sort of reasoning doesn't get us anywhere, Carole. Dinah's been very difficult lately, and we both jumped to the conclusion that she was playing us up—she was, too, but not out of cussedness. She was feeling damned ill.'

Luke turned his attention to Jane. 'It seems as if your

nursing experience is going to come in very useful,' he said
so coolly it was hard to believe that emotional exchange of
their recent confrontation. 'Have you ever nursed a case of
glandular fever before?'

'*I* want to nurse Dinah,' Carole put in fiercely. 'Jane can
show me what to do—and I want to stay with Dinah all the
time, night and day. If you don't mind, Luke, I'm going up
to her now.'

Alone with Luke, Jane was painfully aware of the
unsureness now of the date for leaving Nightingale House.
Once again Fate had stepped in and taken over, and she
could see that the same thoughts were bedevilling Luke.

He said,

'You'd better go up and help Carole—she'll need plenty
of assurance in the days ahead.' He sounded very tired, and
now, in the bright light of the hall, Jane could see the marks
of strain in his face. She wanted to say something—she
wanted to have another attempt at convincing him that her
dealings with Roy Barford were over, but somehow this
didn't seem the right time. His mind was occupied with
other problems; he didn't even seem to notice when she left
him.

The mist lifted sufficiently the following day to let the sun
appear, intermittently at first, but by midday it was clear
enough for the children to play outside, and off they went
with the liveliness of lambs turned out to pasture.

A sample of Dinah's blood had been flown to the
mainland, and until the results came through nothing was
going to stop Carole worrying herself into a frenzy. There
was no need for Dinah to have someone constantly in
attendance, but Carole wouldn't move from her bedside.
Dinah was still restless, but no longer had a high
temperature, as Luke had dosed her with aspirin to bring it
down. Carole was constantly on the watch for any oppor-

tunity to administer to the sick girl, doing unnecessary but
comforting things like wiping her clammy hands and laying
cold compresses on her forehead.

This constant attention worried Jane, who thought Dinah
should be allowed to sleep. Luke had already told his sister-
in-law that there was no treatment for the virus that caused
glandular fever except rest and aspirin in the acute stage,
but all he got for his pains was a reproachful look. Jane
could see that Carole thought neither of them was doing
enough for the sick girl.

When Jane went down to fetch the children in for their
lunch she met Luke going towards the garage and, plucking
up her courage, told him she thought Carole was fussing
over Dinah too much.

'Let her fuss all she wants,' Luke said. 'It's just the
treatment she needs. Surely you remember from your
training that it's just as important to treat the mother as it is
to treat the child? If Carole thinks she's being useful—let
her think it.'

'There's something else,' Jane persisted. 'The mist is
clearing. I phoned the airport, and there's a possibility of
the flights being resumed later this afternoon. I'll leave
whenever you want.'

He stared at her, his expression not giving anything away.
'I think it would be wiser to stay. It looks as if Carole will be
fully occupied with Dinah now, so the whole responsibility
of looking after the children falls on you. By the way, when
you go back in, would you tell Marie I won't be in for
lunch. I'm meeting Dr Reevers, and under the
circumstances I won't invite him back for dinner. Tell
Marie that, too, in case she starts preparing something.'

He was politeness itself, but Jane sensed that the rift
between them was widening, and that hurt, because at last
she had faced up to the fact that she was growing to care for
this man. Why else should what he thought of her matter so

much? When the time came, he would send her out of his life and possibly out of his mind, too, but she would always be a prisoner of her memories.

She went without lunch herself, saying she wanted to use the time trying to master some more of the words in the sign language manuals. Actually she wanted to avoid being alone with Marie, knowing that she wouldn't be able to hide her inner despair from that sharp lady. Later that afternoon she had her first real chance to try out her newly acquired skills.

The mist had dwindled to nothing, though a faint haze still clung to the trees when she gathered the children together and took them on the twenty-minute walk to the nearest beach.

Not all of them opted to go with her. Tracy and Karen had stayed behind for a cookery lesson. Marie was going to teach them to make scones to have with clotted cream and jam for tea. Three of the bigger boys had gone by bus to Hugh Town to buy presents to take home, and Becky, for some reason, wouldn't leave the sick-room.

Paul, the little boy with the pale blond hair, whom Marie in her inimitable manner had dubbed Whitey, walked clinging to Jane's hand, and, though he was as different in looks and character from Jamie as any child could be, the very feel of his hand in hers evoked poignant memories.

Susan and Jamie had been in Los Angeles just a week now. Jim had travelled to California with them and seen them settled in the clinic before returning home. He was trying to build up a practice as an accountant from his home base, and couldn't afford to stay away long, but he had looked like a man drained when he got back to Esher—certainly not fit for work; he had two lots of jet lag to sleep off first. He had promised to phone Jane as soon as he heard anything definite from the clinic—but the long-awaited call had not come yet.

The shore line came into sight—a tiny, rocky bay with a crescent-shaped sandy beach. The children whooped with joy and made a dash to see who could get there first, just as if they had been starved of the sea for years.

A beach is a perfect playground, Jane thought as she settled herself in a hollow with her back against a rock. The children had at once whipped off their shoes and socks, and the ones who didn't mind the cold were paddling. Others were soon well away building a sand-castle, and two of the girls had wandered off to collect sea-shells. They took this very seriously, studying each one—and they had a great variety to choose from—with close attention, discarding any that were chipped or flawed in any way.

It seemed so sad to Jane that these children could not hear the pounding of the sea, or the weening of the gulls, or even the soft soughing of the wind in the trees, yet their other senses were so sharpened that they seemed to gain a greater appreciation of some things than hearing children. For instance—the shells. Watching the two small girls turning their finds over, looking at every detail—even sniffing them—Jane suspected that they appreciated more things about the world about them than hearing children ever did. Whatever the outcome of her stay at Nightingale House, she thought, she had gained something from it. Working with these special children was its own reward.

By the end of the afternoon she felt as if she had mastered the rudiments of basic sign language—at least the children, though not all, could understand what she was trying to say. Her biggest stumbling block was trying to understand them, as they signed so rapidly.

To begin with she tried out words on them that were used most commonly, such as bed—two hands placed under the cheek—and eat—putting the finger to the mouth. The children grinned at her clumsy attempts at first, but they soon took her in hand and put themselves out to teach her, correcting the mistakes she was making.

Stroking imaginary side whiskers indicated a cat, she learnt. Deaf was two fingers to the ear; talk, passing one's fingers to and fro in an alternate action; drink, holding an imaginary glass to the lips; friend, clasping the right hand over the left; love—and here, Whitey took over. He pointed to himself, folded his arms across his chest, and then pointed to Jane. Jane didn't have to refer to the manual to know what that meant—it was only too plain. She scooped Whitey into her arms and hugged him, relishing the feel of his arms around her neck. When she put him on his feet again, she saw Luke watching her.

'I—I didn't know you were there,' she said, blushing with confusion.

'You were too busy to notice—I've been here quite a few minutes.' He eased himself on to the sand, not near as he had on Samson, but nearby. 'Marie told me where I'd find you. I was curious to see how you were managing alone with the children.'

'Not as well as I hoped,' she confessed.

His manner towards her was formal, more businesslike than friendly. 'There are one or two points you must remember when conversing with the deaf. Facial expressions are just as important. There's no need to grimace, but always look sympathetic when enquiring after their well-being or health—it makes it easier for them to understand the nature of the enquiry. All questions should be accompanied by a raising of the eyebrows. Try to express your meaning in your expression as much as you are able—you should find no difficulty with that, you're quite adept at using your eyes.'

Jane wasn't sure whether Luke was being ironic or paying her a compliment. She sighed to herself. She could expect very few compliments from now on.

'Another thing,' he went on, 'when you come to practise

lip-reading, you must remember that its one big drawback is its ambiguity. A number of letters which sound quite different to a person who can hear *look*, to a deaf person, as if they're pronounced with almost the exact same movement of the lips. Common sense will tell you to speak slowly and distinctly, and never in complicated sentences. Use a kind of verbal telegraphese—instead of saying, "I am going", say, "I go". Instead of, "Are you coming?" say, 'You come?", at the same time raising your eyebrows. Get it?'

'Yes,' said Jane, then, greatly daring and with her heart thudding, she added, 'But will I be here long enough to practise all this?'

It was a mistake—she had pressured him too soon; she realised that when she saw his expression harden. 'This is not the time nor place to go into that,' he said, rising to his feet. He offered her a lift up and she found his hand cold to the touch. He clapped several times to get the children's attention. 'Tea,' he said.

Only once on the homeward walk did he speak to Jane again, and that was to say, 'Try and get Becky out of Dinah's room. I don't want her near that sick-room.'

Jane was surprised at his vehemence; she also forgot his dislike of being questioned. 'But why? You don't think there's any danger of her catching glandular fever, do you?'

'Just do as I say,' came the abrupt answer.

The results of Dinah's blood test came the following day. They were positive—the news Carole had prayed for. Gladular fever was nothing to what she had feared, and her whole bearing now changed. She had neglected her appearance in the past two days—she had postponed Dr Reevers' visit, now she dashed off to make amends, leaving Jane in charge of the sick-room.

Jane thought Dinah had every reason to resent her mother's light-heartedness. As she was still feeling so ill herself, she didn't see anything to feel bright about. Jane, who had had glandular fever as a student, knew just what Dinah was suffering—sore throat, lassitude, and aching limbs. She squeezed some oranges, strained the juice into a glass, added ice and took it up to her patient.

'Sip this, you'll find it very soothing,' she said as she propped Dinah against her shoulder and held the glass for her. Dinah sipped warily at first, because she found it so painful to swallow, but the orange juice slipped down, cool and delicious.

'You enjoyed that?' Jane asked, but Dinah didn't feel well enough to admit she was enjoying anything at the moment. Later, however, much to Jane's gratification, she asked for another glass of orange juice. 'It's better than the stuff out of a bottle,' she conceded. 'And this time leave the bits in, I like them.'

Jane felt that a small battle had been won. For the first time Dinah had spoken to her without her usual hostility, and Jane decided to take advantage of that.

She waited until Dinah had finished her second drink, then broached the subject that had been very much on her conscience. 'I feel I ought to grovel to you and beg your pardon,' she said, putting the empty glass on the bedside-table. 'I put you in such an impossible situation over that shoulder-strap affair, and I haven't had a chance to speak to you about it since. I'm so sorry, Dinah. I had no idea Becky would copy what I did, or that it would cause trouble between you and your mother——'

'There's no need for you to apologise to me,' said Dinah gruffly. She looked embarrassed. 'And there's always trouble between me and my mother, anyway——' She stopped herself saying more, remembering the long, painful hours when she had slipped in and out of troubled sleep, and every time she had opened her eyes, her mother had been there by her bed—always there. She felt emotions new to her—a mixture of remorse and shame, and suddenly her eyes filled with tears.

'Why is everyone so nice to me? Why are you *nice* to me? You don't have to be,' she said, with a trace of her former truculence.

Jane smiled. 'I'm just doing my job.' She straightened the bed and punched the pillows to make Dinah more comfortable. 'Would you like me to change your nightie? This has got rather crumpled.'

'Not now—perhaps later.' Dinah's eyes followed Jane as she crossed the room to close the window. A strong wind had sprung up, sweeping away the last remnants of the mist. 'I hated you at first—I resented you coming here. I didn't want strangers—I thought we were all right as we were, just Mum and Luke and me.' Her words came out slowly, as if against her will. 'I was deliberately rude to you—so you don't have to be nice to me. You don't owe me anything.'

Jane turned and looked at her. 'People who are ill, as you've been for some time now, do and say things they don't mean. And, if you *did* mean them, I can understand that, too. I was a stranger—I did intrude into your family circle. But I'm not here for long, so put up with me for a week or two longer, won't you, Dinah? It's much nicer to be friends than—than enemies——'

To Dinah's surprise, the nurse she considered to be always so calm and collected looked as if she was about to cry. In fact, without another word, she bolted from the room. Dinah felt near to tears herself. 'It's all my fault,' she moaned in self-pity. 'I never say the right thing. Nobody understands me. Oh, I wish I was dead!'

But later, when Luke came in and took her temperature and gave her something soothing for her throat, and was so sympathetic in his manner, Dinah changed her opinion. Life was good sometimes—even if only in small patches.

'How long am I going to have this beastly glandular

fever?' she asked him.

Luke wouldn't commit himself. 'That depends. It could drag on for months, but the acute state—that won't last longer than a few days, and I think you're over the worst of it now. I've got an old friend and colleague coming tomorrow—I'll get him to have a look at you. It's always safe to have a second opinion.'

'What's he like—this friend?'

Luke stroked his chin, pretending to consider. 'Let me see, now. He's a widower, he has a son about eighteen, and he's a few years older than me.'

Dinah groaned. 'Oh, not another middle-aged doctor—haven't you got any *young* friends?'

Luke laughed. 'I think I preferred you when you were delirious, it was kinder on my ego,' he said. 'Anyway, your mother asked me to ask you what you'd like for supper?'

'I don't want any supper. I'm full up with two glasses of delicious orange juice which Jane made me.' Dinah raised herself on her elbow and looked at Luke imploringly. 'I'm lonely, Luke. Couldn't little Becky come back? She's company for me.'

Luke shook his head. 'I'm sorry, Dinah, but I've sent her away for her own sake. Glandular fever isn't highly infectious, but I still wouldn't take the risk. Apart from that, Becky has seen enough of sickbeds in her short life, and I don't intend her to get a thing about it. I'll ask Nurse to come and sit with you when she's not occupied with the children.'

It was only later that Dinah wondered why he should refer to Jane as Nurse—the first time he had ever done so.

Carole looked forward with great relish to Scott Reever's visit; it was something that would put her on her mettle. The last two days had been a nightmare from which she had emerged still bearing the brunt. Now she could occupy herself with happier thoughts, such as planning a special dish for dinner, but Luke vetoed that.

'Scott prefers plain food—no *nouvelle cuisine* for him. He'd rather get on and eat, not just sit and admire the plate!'

'I thought about lobster Thermidor——'

'Just plain lobster and salad. Lobster freshly caught is a treat in itself.'

So dinner that night was lobster served with new potatoes the size of walnuts, crisp salad, French bread and Cornish butter. Jane took to Dr Reevers at once; he had a friendly, homely manner that put her instantly at her ease.

He was medium height and inclined to stoutness, and had the ruddy complexion of a farmer—not Jane's concept of a psychiatrist, whom she always thought of as lean and spare and scholarly-looking. Invariably, the conversation at the dinner-table turned to Becky. Scott had spent some time with both Becky and Dinah that afternoon.

He said now that he found Becky a normal, well-balanced, happy little girl, and if she preferred playing with her toys to playing with companions of her own age, that trait was not uncommon in only children.

'What about her mutism? Is it due to psychological factors, in your opinion?' Luke asked.

'I wouldn't like to be dogmatic about that. Personally, I don't think so. Becky seems too well-adjusted to have any hang-ups, but I'm not saying that she didn't at one time. This obsession with tying similar toys together, pretending that one is the mother and one the baby, indicates to me that at some time in her short life she went through the trauma of being parted from her mother. She could have been very young at the time, a few months even, and the distress of that parting lies buried in her psyche. She's found her own way of dealing with it—so I shouldn't look upon it as a problem, it's more of a therapy. And, another thing——' he looked at them all in turn from under his bushy eyebrows, and his eyes gleamed as mischievously as any schoolboys '—I'm willing to take on a bet with any of you that one day she's going to surprise you by coming out with something spontaneous.'

'You mean she'll say something—she'll actually *speak*?' cried Carole, amazed.

'I think that's expecting too much. I meant a sound—a laugh, perhaps. She smiles a lot—laughter could follow, and once Becky feels the vibration from her vocal chords, she'll attempt other sounds.' He flashed a good-humoured look in Luke's direction. 'Of course, if I knew more about her past I could be more specific about her future, but my colleague here is a very cagey fellow. He only tells me what he wants me to know. I believe he knows a lot more about Becky's past than he has admitted—about her parents, for instance. I can't understand the reason for all this mystery.'

Luke didn't answer immediately. He was playing with a small pile of salt that had been spilt on the tablecloth, pushing it into patterns with his finger. When he did speak, it was in an offhand manner. 'Perhaps I am being a little over-cautious, but I have good reasons. When the time is ripe I'll tell you all I know about Becky, but until then I'm afraid you'll have to contain your curiosity.' He was addressing no one specifically, yet Jane had the uncanny feeling that his words were aimed at her.

Carole moved restlessly, anxious to bring the subject on to Dinah. 'What did you think of my invalid?' she asked. 'Do you agree with Luke that it isn't serious?'

Scott gave her a reassuring smile. 'I certainly don't agree that it isn't serious, and I don't believe my old pal said any such thing. It's not serious in as much as it isn't fatal, but it's a pretty rotten thing to have, anyway. But you've nothing to worry about, Mrs Springer. Dinah is a very sick girl at present, but she'll recover—and in the meantime she's in very good hands. Don't you agree with me, Luke, that you and Jane make a very good team?'

Luke looked at Jane, his blue eyes completely without guile. 'I couldn't ask for a more trustworthy and reliable helpmate,' he said, which made the others smile appreciatively, but which gave Jane no satisfaction. She knew how hollow his words were.

CHAPTER SEVEN

EVERY other Saturday was change-over day. A day of excitement and a day of anxiety; a time of joy and a time for tears—and always a pull on the heart-strings for all concerned. For one lot of children were leaving, and another lot arriving.

Early that Saturday afternoon, Jane and Carole and Marie stood in the drive and waved the children off—and at every window of the minibus bobbing heads and a flurry of hands appeared, waving frantically in return.

Carole took out her handkerchief and blew her nose. 'I'd better go up and see how Dinah is,' she said huskily. 'I've neglected her shamefully all morning.' And she returned to the house, followed by an ominously silent Marie.

Jane felt lost. Now that the children were gone, the place seemed uncannily quiet—a quietness that was suddenly shattered by the sound of a telephone ringing.

'It's for you!' Marie shouted. Being requested by Jane not to call her Miss Peters, she now called her nothing, thinking it disrespectful to address a nurse by her christian name. Jane went cold. It was Roy—it had to be Roy. Every time the phone went, her heart skipped a beat. She dreaded a call from him, but at the same time could not help wondering why he had not been in touch with her before. This time she was again reprieved—it was a call from her brother-in-law.

'Jim! It's good to hear from you. Have you got any news for me?'

Jim sounded rather down. 'Sue phoned a short while ago

106

to tell me the preliminary tests on Jamie have been completed, and everything's OK, but now there's a complication; the operation is being postponed, as Jamie has developed a slight chest infection. It's nothing to worry about, Jane. Sue stressed that, but I could tell she was worried, all the same. Have you received her card? Well, there's one in the post for you. She says you'll know why she hasn't had time to write you a letter.'

Jane replaced the receiver with a feeling of anticlimax. At least Erik Tollesbury had not refused to undertake the operation—everything was all right as far as that went; it was just unfortunate that Jamie should have picked up this infection at the last moment. But it could happen in any hospital. It was one of the things nurses on surgical wards dreaded—that and enteritis.

Jane went upstairs to strip the beds and remake them for the new occupants. She was glad of something to keep her busy and her mind occupied. So many anxieties crowded in upon her these days—Roy Barford, Jamie, the money to pay for his operation—and, above all, the constant nagging reminder of Luke's mistrust of her.

In the company of others, his manner towards her, though it lacked the old spontaneity, was always very correct, but alone with her he treated her with a veiled suspicion, making her ever conscious that those watchful blue eyes monitored every movement she made.

This made her so uneasy, she could never be her natural self when with him, and he gave her very little opportunity to be on her own. Checking up on me, she thought. Making sure I don't get another chance to search his desk. There had been no further mention of secretarial work—Luke was making sure she had no excuse to use his study, either.

She emerged from the dormitories just as Carole appeared from Dinah's room laden with an armful of cat.

'Guess where I found Mitzi?' she cried. 'On Dinah's

bed! She's been making a habit of climbing up the cherry tree and in through the window. The last thing I want is for her to have her kittens in Dinah's room—but, would you believe, Dinah's quite tickled by the idea!'

'She's lonely,' said Jane.

'And bored. Now that she's so much better she hates staying in her room. I do think Luke could let her come down now. Don't you think he's being a teeny-weeny bit over-cautious?'

'It's for your sake, Carole.'

Carole sighed. 'I did over-react about Dinah at first, didn't I? To be honest, I was neurotic—but I'll have a word with Luke when he gets back. In the meantime I'd better take this fat lump to the wash-house and lock her in. A new lot of her dreadeds will be arriving soon.'

They went down the stairs together and then parted, Jane going on to the kitchen. There, to her amazement, she found Marie perched on the stool she used when ironing, puffing away at a cigarette—not smoking, just puffing—she didn't know how to inhale properly. She glared at Jane defiantly.

'I suppose you're shocked, seeing me smoke?'

'I'm not shocked, but I am surprised. I didn't know you enjoyed a cigarette.'

'I'm *not* enjoying it!' Marie resented the very idea. 'It's either this or howl my eyes out, and I don't want to cry and have Mrs Springer find me with my eyes all red.'

Jane crossed the floor to her. 'Marie—what's upset you?'

'The kids leaving of course. I—I kinda get used to them, and then they have to go and leave me. I really took a shine to that little Whitey.' Marie blinked rapidly several times. 'Darn this smoke, it's got in my eyes. He promised to write, but of course he won't. They never do. They get home to their mums and forget all about old Marie.'

The time Marie didn't bother to blink, but let her eyes water instead. With a practised air she flicked the cigarette into a a sink, where it sizzled and went out. 'I should have married and had kids of my own, then I wouldn't have felt this wrench every time, but I never seemed to get round to thinking about marriage when I was young. I came over to Scilly for a holiday about thirty years ago, and stayed on—earning my keep one way or another. There's a great demand for domestics in the holiday season, and I got by in the winter helping with the flower trade. Now I've got this steady job, and thank my lucky stars for it because I've got a good home as well—but nothing comes cheap, and I pay ever time the kids leave.'

'There'll be another lot of children arriving shortly,' Jane reminded her gently.

'Yes—and that means I must start on the tea. They'll arrive as hungry as hunters—they always do.'

Jane, crossing the hall shortly afterwards, heard the familiar, tuneless whistling that heralded Marie at work. Obviously she had successfully put her troubled heart into cold storage for another two weeks.

On Saturdays, during the season, the *Scillonian* made two trips, the second time docking at the quay just after four o'clock, bringing over today the fresh intake of children for Nightingale House. The outward-bound children were travelling on the return journey to Penzance in the care of voluntary helpers, to be met there by parents or relatives, anxious for their reunion.

Carole usually helped Luke with the change-over, as it was too much for one person to handle, but today Scott had offered to take her place, leaving her free should Dinah need her. Carole told Jane this when she came in from shutting Mitzi in the wash-house.

'Will Dr Reevers be coming back with Luke?' Jane asked.

In response to this question Carole gave what Jane could only describe to herself as a self-conscious smile.

'Well, actually, he won't. You see, I'm meeting him later

in Hugh Town, and we're having dinner together. Jane,' Carole hesitated, 'you like Scott, don't you?'

'I think he's really charming.'

'Yes, he is, and kind, too. Do you think it's foolish of me—well, you know—to get ideas about him?' Carole's usual composure having temporarily deserted her, she was unsure of herself. 'I can't be sure how he feels about me, he's so charming to everybody.'

'Yes, but he doesn't watch everybody all the time as he does you—he can't take his eyes off you. And why do you think he's extended his stay on St Mary's—to be with Luke?'

Carole glowed—her eyes, her face, her smile all glowed. 'Oh, Jane, I can't believe that only a few days ago when Dinah was so ill I felt in the depths of despair. Now I feel on top of the world. Be happy for me, Jane.'

Be happy for me. Jane stood, watching Carole tripping lightly up the stairs. Be happy for me, too, she thought. I need it. And following that troubled thought came another—even more troubling, in its way. If Carole was dining out, that mean't she and Luke would have supper tête-à-tête. Alone, in that big, empty dining-room, facing each other across the table with nobody else there to ease the tension! She knew she couldn't face it.

But once the fresh group of children arrived she was kept too busy to worry about the immediate future—the present was about as much as she could cope with. She watched the new intake alight from the minibus with a feeling akin to panic. How was she ever going to converse with these strange children, given her limited knowledge of sign language? But when she saw that the children were just as worried as she was—perhaps even more so,—her own anxiety disappeared beneath a wave of sympathy and understanding for them.

What must it be like for these young folk coming tired

and travel-stained into this house of strangers—into this silent, unfamiliar world where nobody knew them? She didn't need language of any kind to show her feelings for them then. She stood with her arms wide, embracing them all with a warm smile of welcome, and they responded by crowding around, chattering at her with their fingers.

It was Becky who came to her assistance. With a self-confidence far beyond her seven years, she slipped easily into the role of hostess and led the way to the kitchen to introduce them to Marie, whose own particular welcome and the laden table were enough to overcome the doubts of the most faint-hearted.

Among the new visitors was a girl about Becky's age with large, slightly protuberant pale blue eyes, and in no time at all Marie had dubbed her Bubbles. It was soon obvious she was going to fill the gap in Marie's heart that Whitey had left. Jane wondered how often the spare, big-hearted woman would have to take refuge in a cigarette before she got hardened to these comings and goings.

Both Carole and Luke had been witnesses to Jane's welcome to the children, standing well back and not interfering, waiting to see how she could manage on her own. When the party had gone on to the kitchen, Carole gave a long-drawn-out sigh. 'Well, what do you make of that? Wasn't Jane marvellous? She's a real natural. I was wondering how *I* was going to cope—the poor kids looked so down-hearted—but Jane took it all in her stride.'

'They had had a rough crossing, and the little ones were homesick. Yes, Jane managed all right.'

'*All right*? That's the understatement of the year! What's the matter with you, Luke? It's not like you to be so grudging with your praise. Jane's a treasure, and you know it. You'd be a fool to let her go.'

Luke took his time answering. He appeared weary, rather as if his energy had drained away. 'She's got her own life to lead,' he said finally.

'Is there a man in her life?'

'What difference does that make?'

'Oh, Luke, don't be so obtuse! Is there someone she has to go back to?'

Again that hesitation, then, 'Yes. I rather believe there is.'

'Oh.' Carole looked disappointed. She changed the subject. 'Couldn't Dinah come downstairs this evening? She's getting so fed up staying in her room all the time. You said yourself the risk of infection is minimal, and now that her temperature's back to normal it wouldn't do her any harm. Couldn't she have supper with you and Jane? You know I'll be out for the evening.'

'Yes, Scott reminded me.' When Luke smiled in that way he looked so much like her husband that Carole's heart flipped over. Dear Ned, she had been faithful to his memory for six years, and he would be the first to understand that she couldn't go on forever with this loneliness bearing down on her. 'Do you approve?' she asked.

'Approve of you and Scott having dinner together? I think it's a great idea. Go off and enjoy yourself, Carole, and forget Dinah—she'll be all right. And of course she may join us for supper, I'll send Jane up to tell her.'

Bedtime was put forward that evening. The children were ready for it after the long, eventful journey, and Jane stayed with them until they had settled down, then she looked in to see if Becky was also asleep. She was, soundly, with a knitted kangaroo clasped tightly in her arms. 'What, no baby?' Jane asked herself, wondering if Becky had given up the habit—but no. She had stuffed a model of a giraffe from a toy zoo into the kangaroo's pouch. Jane couldn't see the connection, but it must have meant something to Becky, for she smiled in her sleep. Jane stooped and kissed her, then went on to Dinah's room to help her prepare for supper.

During the height of her fever Dinah had been an easy patient to nurse, grateful for anything anyone could do to ease her discomfort, but now that she felt better she was inclined to lapse into her old fretful ways if the mood took her, and she was feeling in a very unhelpful mood this evening.

'I thought you would be pleased about joining us downstairs,' said Jane as she helped Dinah into a pair of jeans a size too small for her.

'What? Just for supper and then back to bed again?' Dinah complained pettishly. 'Not even being allowed to stay up and watch television—I don't call that much of a treat! I don't want to eat with you and Luke, either—I'd rather be with Marie, she's more fun.'

Jane secretly sympathised with these sentiments—there was no fun between herself and Luke any longer. Just suspicion on his part and caution on hers.

She fetched Dinah's hairbrush from the dressing-table. 'Let me do something about your hair,' she suggested. 'I don't think it's even had a comb through it today.'

Dinah's hair was stubborn like its owner, but Jane persevered, brushing it until Dinah's scalp tingled, and several time she gave an exaggerated 'O-ow', but at last it was free of tangles, and as smooth as curly hair could be smoothed. It was the colour of rich, clear honey, but Dinah eyed her reflection with dissatisfaction.

'I wish I had hair like yours,' she said unexpectedly. 'Soft and silky and shiny.'

Jane was touched by this tribute. 'And when I was young I would have given my eye-teeth for curls. I still would—I think curls are softening to the face.'

'Nothing would soften my hair—it's as tough as steel wool.'

'Oh, what a saddo we are tonight.' Jane laughed. 'Dinah, you've got lovely hair, it just needs taking care of, that's all. If you had it thinned out and styled, you'd find it would be more manageable. When you feel well enough, perhaps you'd let me take you to the hairdressers?'

Dinah glared accusingly at Jane though the mirror. 'There you go—being nice to me again.'

'As I told you before, it goes with the job,' said Jane.

There was quiche and ham and cold chicken for supper, and salads from the delicatessen in the town where Marie had shopped that morning—she had little time for cooking on change-over day. These were put out on the sideboard, together with a selection of cheeses and dry biscuits for Jane, Luke and Dinah to help themselves.

Dinah took two dry biscuits, spread them thinly with butter, and topped each with a slice of tomato. 'Is that your supper!' Luke enquired drily.

'You can't expect me to get hungry when all I do is lie abed all day!' Dinah retorted.

'Pity, because I thought of taking you for a drive tomorrow to Old Town Bay, provided the weather keeps fine. But there's no point in making plans if you're not eating—you won't be strong enough. There's no sustenance in two biscuits.'

Dinah started to gobble her food. 'This is only my starters—wait until you see my main course. I haven't even begun to eat yet.'

Ten minutes later, Luke said, 'There's no need to make a pig of yourself—there's enough on your plate for two.'

Dinah glared. 'There's no satisfying you!' She spoke with difficulty, her mouth being full.

In a wry kind of way Jane was enjoying this little conversation, grateful to Dinah for taking the spotlight off herself. Once Jane caught Luke staring at her, and was disconcerted by his cool, unblinking blue gaze. What was he thinking behind that masklike expression? Did he still condemn her in his heart, or was he by now making excuses for her? His expression gave nothing away.

Strangely, Dinah put up no opposition when Luke reminded her it was time to go back to bed—in fact, she seemed ready to go. She was weaker than she cared to admit even to herself. After helping her undress, Jane went to her own room. She felt restless. It was a beautiful evening—too good to spend watching television. Marie was already watching an old Hollywood weepy, with a handkerchief at the ready, and a bag of sweets on her lap. Jane didn't want to spoil her enjoyment. She stood at the window, staring at the sea and the off-shore islands, sharp and clear in the unpolluted atmosphere—a perfect evening for a walk.

She changed her blouse for a jumper, as the evenings got chilly once the sun went down; there was always a breeze on Scilly. She put on a pair of trainers and her white anorak with the red piping, then tied her scarlet scarf over her hair and knotted it under the chin.

She had seen nothing of Luke since supper, but that wasn't unusual—he spent most of his evenings in his study doing paperwork. Tonight was an exception, for when she emerged from the house he was coming from the stables driving the Spitfire. He stopped when he saw her. 'Want a lift to Hugh Town?' he said casually.

'Actually, I was going for a walk.'

'Anywhere in particular?'

'No—no—just a—a walk.' Jane wished she could for once get over her nervousness of him and speak naturally.

'Then perhaps I could make a suggestion. There's a good walk around the Garrison, and you haven't been to that part of the town yet. Would you have any objection if I joined you? There's likely to be a fine sunset tonight, and the view from the Garrison is spectacular.'

'But wouldn't that interfere with your plans?'

'I hadn't planned anything,' he answered curtly. He opened the passenger door for her, and Jane slipped in beside him, a prey to mixed feelings. The pleasure of being in his company in this informal setting was offset by the thought that this was the first time they had really been alone since that awful afternoon in his study, and he might now take the opportunity to tell her it was time she packed her bags and left.

She knew she had stayed on on sufferance because of Dinah's illness, but Dinah no longer needed her. True, that left the children to consider, the main reason for her coming to Nightingale House in the first place, but surely out of all those applications Luke had received he would be able to find someone to replace her? And Jane argued like this to herself all the way on the silent drive to Hugh Town.

Luke drove on and up the hill through the Garrison Gate and parked just the other side. From here it was quite a steep climb—at least for Jane, who wasn't used to so much exercise. They continued past the old powder-house, on up the hill skirting the sixteenth-century castle that was now a hotel, then right towards the forts. They could see the islands of St Agnes and Gugh and Annet, the home of puffins in summer, and the sea in St Mary's Sound, moving gently like rippled silk. It was so still, so quiet, that the tolling of the bell-buoy which marked the Spanish Ledges could be heard above the cries of the gulls.

Soon they came to a promontory enclosed by a granite wall where two old cannon pointed out to sea. There was no one else around, other evening strollers had continued along the coastal road, taking the circular route back to town. Luke leant against the ramparts staring moodily out to sea like a man with a problem. Jane ran her hand along the barrel of the nearest cannon, touching history—thinking back to the old days when these guns had been installed as a precaution against invaders, and as a protection from pirates and privateers.

The sky was on fire—a brilliant panorama of red and gold

that marked the passing of the dying sun. Jane joined Luke
at the ramparts, leaning on her elbows against the wall,
drinking in the beauty all around her—two silent watchers,
together, but miles apart. The brilliant colours diffused and
faded into the pastel hues of lilac and saffron, spreading an
afterglow of silver light that turned to gold where it touched
the sea, throwing into black relief the two low hills on
Samson.

Luke broke the long silence. 'It's traditional,' he said, 'to
watch the sun set over Samson.'

'It's beautiful,' said Jane, unable to find words to describe
her true feelings. She felt tearful, not because of the sunset,
but because for the first time in days Luke had spoken to
her not unkindly.

'Watch,' he said. 'It's not over.'

The sun had gone, leaving a pale green cloudless sky and
a long sparkling pathway on the sea that shimmered like
molten gold. Jane felt her senses enhanced by nature's
bounty. It heightened her perception of things around her,
made her increasingly aware of the man beside her—aware
of him in the sense that he meant so much to her.

'I'll never forget this evening,' she said spontaneously. 'It
will be something to remember when I get home.'

Luke shifted his weight from one foot to the other. It was
too dark now to see his face clearly, only the glitter of his
eyes was noticeable in the reflected light from the sunset.

'That's what I wanted to discuss with you. When are you
going home?'

'I—I've been waiting for *you* to tell *me*. That was the
arrangement, wasn't it? You were going to think things
over?'

'Yes, and I've done a lot of thinking in the past few days.
I really don't know what to make of you. Carole said you
were a natural with the children, and I'm inclined to think
that, too, and for that reason I'm reluctant to let you

go. But can I trust you? That's what I keep asking myself. Can I believe your story—somehow it doesn't quite ring true.' He paused, and Jane waited, her heart thudding, feeling that nothing she said would dispel his doubts, as he had already made up his mind about her.

He considered his words carefully. 'What I wanted to ask you is—were your sister and brother-in-law in on this pact you made with the *Moonraker*?'

'No—of course not. I thought I made that clear!'

'You didn't—and, if they weren't in the know, why not? Why didn't you tell them?'

Jane tried to stem the feeling that the ground was slipping away beneath her. The light was quickly fading, and in the shadows Luke loomed larger than life, an accusing figure towering over her. The words she wanted to say stuck in her throat.

'They wouldn't have agreed to such a plan, would they?' Luke's voice was harsh, challenging.

'No—no, they wouldn't.'

'So you went ahead behind their backs, and made this deal on your own? That doesn't say much for your trustworthiness, does it?'

'I—I did it for Jamie. I was grasping straws, I would have done anything to save him.'

'And how are you going to save him now—now that you've forfeited the fee for the story of my life?' His voice was loaded with sarcasm.

Jane's shoulders sagged. 'I'll raise a loan on my house.'

'You could have done that in the first place.'

'Yes, I suppose so.' Jane was too heart-sick, too tired, to argue further.

Luke moved suddenly, taking her by surprise, gripping her hard by the shoulders. 'Tell me—was it only the money? Wasn't it for another reason too?'

'I don't understand what you mean!'

'Some woman will do anything for love,' he said bitterly.

Jane started to laugh, a laugh that threatened to turn to tears any minute. 'You don't think—you can't think that I love—*love* Roy Barford?'

His hands dropped to his side; he went suddenly very still. 'Did you say Roger Barford?'

'*Roy* Barford—the editor of the *Moonraker*—I thought I told you his name.'

'No, you didn't—but it's of no consequence.' His voice was clipped, unnatural-sounding. Across the water came the monotonous tolling of the bell-buoy, and Luke gave a long, troubled sigh.

'Let's leave it like that, then,' he said wearily. 'You'll work out your month here, and we'll have no more of these fruitless discussions.'

CHAPTER EIGHT

EARLY the following afternoon, Jane took her writing case, her sun-glasses, and a reclining chair into the garden, with every intention of writing to Susan.

Not counting Becky, she was the only one still on the premises. Luke, at the wheel of the minibus, had driven Carole and Dinah off to Old Town Beach as he had promised. Dinah looked blooming—whether it was the prospect of going on a little trip alone with her own family, or whether she had resorted to a little artifice, Jane couldn't be sure, but the girl certainly looked well. Nobody would guess from her looks that she had anything wrong with her. She looked attractive, too, in a simple pink and grey dress, and she had folded a grey chiffon scarf into a bandeau and tied it round her head to keep her hair in place. In spite of this precaution, a few curly tendrils had escaped and the way they coiled about her face suited her—and she knew it!

Carole was in good spirits, too, obviously very happy, a legacy from the night before when she had returned home still savouring the hours she had spent in Scott's company. Luke was the odd one out—there was nothing cheerful or happy about him. He looked like a man who had not slept for days, and the laughter lines around his eyes had been replaced by deep lines of worry. Even when Becky had reached up on tiptoe to kiss him goodbye—she had been invited to join them on the outing, but had refused, preferring to stay home with her 'family', her assortment of stuffed toys—he had returned the kiss in an absent-minded way. Marie had marshalled the children together and taken them on their first visit to the beach, and now Jane relaxed in the long chair in a sunny corner of the garden.

She was wearing the yellow dress Marie had fetched from the cleaners the previous day—a dress that was meaningful to Jane as Luke had complimented her on it. That was the day she had arrived at Nightingale House full of foreboding—fears that had been amply justified since.

The writing-pad slipped from her fingers on to the grass as drowsiness stole over her. She had slept little the night before, and when she had escaped from troubled thoughts into a shallow unconsciousness it was only to be haunted by dreams that did more harm than sleeplessness did. Now, with eyes closed and on the edge of oblivion, she was unaware that Scott had come round the side of the house and had paused, admiring the sight of a pretty girl sunning herself. Her thick dark hair fell loose over her shoulders, and her brown arms and legs were bare. An attractive girl—a very desirable-looking girl, Scott thought, but only, he understood, a summer visitor, and he wondered if that was partly the reason for Luke's varying moods.

Jane stirred and realised that her writing-pad had gone. Leaning over to pick it up, she spotted Scott and immediately sat up, pulling her skirt down over her knees. Scott came across to her.

'Am I disturbing you?'

'No—I wasn't sleeping, just lazing. I meant to write letters, but felt too lazy to do that even.'

'An afternoon like this is meant for lazing in.' Scott lowered himself on the lawn beside her. 'Where's everybody? I called at the house, but nobody was in. Are you on your own?'

'No, Becky is around somewhere. The others are all out—Marie has given up her free day to get acquainted with the new lot of children, and Luke, Carole and Dinah have gone for a run. Could I make you a cup of tea?'

'Not tea, but if there's a beer in the fridge, I wouldn't say no—I've just walked up from Hugh Town. Perhaps you'll join me?'

Jane rose from her chair, taking her writing-pad with her—there'd be no letters written today now. She found the kitchen cool and dark after the glare of the garden. There was a large can of lager in the fridge, and she took it with two glasses back to where Scott was sitting. Jane never felt shy with Scott. At first she had treated him with the deference she felt due to his position, but he had soon put an end to that, insisting she called him by his first name. She had been Jane to him from the moment of introduction.

He watched her from where he lay, lolling on the grass, preferring the ground to one of the chairs available, as she carefully measured out the lager, giving most of it to him, keeping just a small drink for herself.

'You're not a proper beer-drinker,' he teased, a few moments later. 'I can tell by the way you're sipping it in that dainty fashion. You should down it like this.' And he finished his drink off in two or three gulps. He wore an old, battered hat tilted over his eyes as protection from the sun. 'Phew, it's going to be a scorcher—not unexpected after that fantastic sunset last night. Did you see the sunset?'

'Yes—I saw the sunset,' said Jane, thinking back to that magic moment with Luke on the ramparts when there had still been hope in her heart that things might come right between them. Her hopes had died with the afterglow. Luke's mood had changed, and this morning he had barely acknowledged her—had driven away without as much as a look in her direction.

Scott pushed his hat back from his eyes. 'I've been hoping for an opportunity to talk with you, ever since I found out you trained at Ben's. How is the old place these days?'

The next few minutes were spent in reminiscing—Jane about her student days, and Scott about his time there as a medical registrar. Memories sparked off other thoughts, and Scott looked about him in a contemplative manner. 'This is a beautiful spot—I envy Luke this set-up. I must admit I was sceptical when I first heard of his plans for a holiday home for deaf children—I couldn't see the connection with the work he used to do for the Home Office. You do know, of course, that he was a forensic pathologist?'

'Yes,' said Jane quietly.

'He still is, of course. He could go back any time he liked, but I don't think he will—not now. He finds this kind of work far more to his liking—he was very restless that last year at the Home Office. Did you know him in those days?'

Jane shook her head. In the true sense of the word she had not known Luke then. An impression of someone—even a powerful impression—wasn't actually knowing them.

'He was brilliant at his job—he could have got to the top of his profession if he had stuck it out. But a combination of things put him off, and about four years ago he chucked it all up and went to live in Tuscany. We lost touch, and it's only this week we've picked up where we left off.' Scott felt in the mood to talk, and who better to talk to than this dark-eyed girl with her quiet air of discretion?'

Jane's quiet air was deceptive; there was nothing quiet about the state of her mind at that moment. She had a sudden premonition that Scott held the key to many things that had puzzled her, and now she didn't want to know about them. Knowing too much about Luke would be like betraying him all over again, and she had already paid the price for that once. But there was no way to stop Scott telling her, and he had only spoken a few sentences before Jane realised that she couldn't stop listening now if she tried.

'He had three rotten years in a row,' Scott said. 'First his eldest brother died—that hit him hard, as it was so unexpected. The following year came the news that his younger brother was ill—that was the brother living in Italy—and the year after that his own health cracked up—nothing serious, he'd been working too hard. He didn't spare himself, and I think the trouble was nothing more than a severe attack of nervous exhaustion—a breakdown, if you prefer. He also had some nasty cases to deal with that year, and one in particular got under his skin. It concerned a young man, twenty or twenty-one, who had murdered his girlfriend. A rather gruesome murder, by all accounts, and it was Luke's evidence that put the chap away for life. That verdict was the end as far as Luke was concerned.'

'But if it was a particularly nasty murder and the man was guilty . . . ?'

'Luke always maintained that the defendant's counsel should have put in a plea of diminished responsibility. But he didn't. He replied on young—what was his name? I'm usually good at remembering names—Bartley, Bardney—I've got it—Barford. Yes, Roger Barford, that's it. He had a water-tight alibi and the defence relied on that. But Luke and the inspector in charge of the case demolished the alibi between them——' Scott broke off, looking up at Jane questioningly.

'You gave a violent shudder just then—are you cold?'

'No—somebody just walked over my grave.' It was an excuse Jane often fell back on when in difficulty. Her mouth was so dry, she drained the last few drops of liquid at the bottom of her glass. 'Why did Luke think there was a case for diminished responsibility?'

'Because young Barford had no record of violence. He lived a pretty aimless life—gambling, playing around. I think he had an older brother who supported him. He had had rheumatic fever as a child, which had left him with a dicky heart, and he made that an excuse for not working. He loved the girl, there was no doubt about that, but when he discovered she'd cheated on him he lost control of himself and went into a kind of frenzy. If he had confessed all to the police then, he would have got off with a lighter sentence, but he didn't. He went to great lengths to cover up his tracks—or else somebody else did it for him. The girl had been stabbed several times; there was blood all over her clothes and the inside of her car—that's where the attack took place. Barford was the prime suspect, in spite of his alibi, and a search was made of his flat and some of his clothes were taken away for examination. The inspector was suspicious of one particular suit that had just come back from the cleaners. When Luke examined it he found signs that stains of some kind had recently been removed, but there wasn't sufficient evidence to connect them with the murdered girl. Luke felt that if it was possible to get a sample of the fluid that had been used in the dry-cleaning process, he might find something incriminating in that.

'A bit of clever detective work on the part of the chief inspector and his team produced the cleaning fluid, and Luke's hunch paid off—there were traces of blood in the fluid which were identified as belonging to the same bloodgroup as the victim, and when confronted with this evidence, Roger Barford broke down and confessed. He was given a life sentence, and his brother was charged with perjury—but *he* was either lucky or had a good lawyer, because he got off with a suspended sentence. By that time, Luke had chucked up his job and gone off to join his brother in Tuscany. I went to the airport to see him off. He was in very low spirits and looked a very sick man, or so I thought. That's why I couldn't believe my eyes when we met again this week. He's a different person—if anything, he looks younger, and so fit—Scilly obviously agrees with him. But there's something on his mind. Have you ever noticed that he loses himself at times—lapses into a state almost bordering on melancholy? It doesn't last. I suppose we all have our secret worries,' Scott added philosophically.

There was no answer. Scott looked at Jane and saw that she was miles away in a world of her own. His first impression of her as glowing with health gave way to a feeling that that was only on the surface. Underneath he sensed a very troubled girl. For one thing, her eyes were ringed by shadows, and a pallor showed through her tan. He wondered what was on her mind now to bring such a hunted look to those wistful eyes.

Jane was now realising the full significance of Luke's query about Roy's name. It seemed unlikely that he had connected the name Barford with the editor of the *Moonraker* before last night—it was not a paper Luke was likely to read. Whatever his suspicions of her before, they must be twofold now—thinking of her in collusion with Roy, part of a scheme to settle an old score. Roy blamed Luke for his brother's heavy sentence, and had nursed plans of revenge for four long years. Only a man sick in his mind could have borne a grudge so long—but wasn't Roy sick? To go to such lengths to get her in Luke's employ as an instrument of revenge—were they the actions of a sane man? Despising him as much as she did, Jane could also feel a certain pity, for he had one trait in his favour—loyalty to his brother, and possibly love, too.

She wondered why she hadn't read or heard about Roger Barford's trial at the time, but, thinking back, it must have taken place during her first year at St Benedict's—a particularly difficult time for her, as that was when she had had glandular fever and had been still trying to keep up with her studies. The Barford case would have been small beer compared with some that caught the headlines, and Jane hadn't had much time that year for reading newspapers or watching television.

The bitter irony about the whole thing, she now realised, was that Luke had nothing to hide—nothing in the way of a scandal in his past to make into a sensational story for Roy's paper. Nothing to hide? she repeated to herself, pulling her thoughts up short. Could she be certain of that? She remembered the photograph of the girl called Kirsty Brownlow and her possible link with Becky, and felt with a sinking heart that she must have unearthed something from Luke's past that day in his study.

'Come back, Jane—come back from wherever you are.'

Jane looked startled at Scott's words; she had almost forgotten his presence. He was looking at her with deep concern in his kind grey eyes.

'Troubled thoughts?' he queried.

Jane felt her throat go tight with unshed tears. One word of sympathy and she knew the floodgates would open. Oh, the relief if she could give way to tears! And relief, too, if she could confide in this understanding man, but that would be another kind of betrayal. She managed an apology for a smile. 'There's nothing more on my mind than a bad conscience,' she said, but she didn't convince Scott.

He smiled. 'Nothing will make me believe you have a guilty conscience; you look far too innocent for that.'

The sudden appearance of Becky made a welcome diversion, as far as Jane was concerned. Becky was clasping a toy Jane hadn't seen before—a tiny black kitten that looked as if it was made out of plush.

Scott sat up, pushed his hat to the back of his head and chuckled. 'I've never seen that child yet unless she's lugging some toy rabbit or pig or teddy bear around with her. But never a doll, I notice—what's she got against dolls?' He suddenly stiffened. 'Good heavens, that's not a toy—it's *real*! It moved—come on, we'd better investigate this.'

He was on his feet in an instant, and Jane quickly followed. Becky ran up to them, her face luminous with joy, holding out for them to see what she was carrying—it was a tiny new-born kitten.

Scott gave an exclamation. 'Jane! That poor thing has only just been born—you can see by the mucus. Where the dickens did Becky find it? Have you got any stray cats around? Any pregnant cats?

Jane stared back at him with glazed eyes. 'Only Carole's Mitzi—but she's pure Siamese!'

A slow, amused smile spread across Scott's homely features. 'Then the most likely explanation is that Mitzi has mated below her—with a non-pedigree moggy!'

'But she can't have! She was sent to the mainland to be mated with another Siamese—at a terrific fee, according to Marie.'

Scott answered with a shout of laughter. 'Then Mitzi must have had her little fling before she was officially mated. It must be a case of superfecundation, and the husband she chose for herself triumphed. Will Carole be upset?' He could hardly speak for laughing, and Jane found his laughter infectious. What a relief it was to laugh when just a few moments ago she had been near to tears.

Gently, she coaxed the kitten away from Becky, who was reluctant to part with it. 'I think the quicker we return this poor little thing to its mother, the better,' she said. 'I know where to find her—in the old wash-house, but I don't know how Becky found out. Carole thought she'd kept Mitzi's hiding-place a secret.'

But the wash-house proved to be empty, and the cat basket showed no signs of having been recently occupied. Becky, who had followed closely on their heels, now watched their efforts to locate the missing cat with such a self-satisfied smirk that it was obvious they were wasting their time. 'I think we'd save ourselves a lot of trouble if we asked Becky where to find her,' Scott suggested.

Jane did so, mouthing her words very carefully, but Becky chose not to understand, and stared back at Jane with guileless blue eyes.

Without hesitation, Jane went into sign language. Rocking her arms for 'baby', stroking imaginary whiskers for 'cat', dropping both hands down, keeping the two first fingers stiff for 'dead', spelling the word 'without' on her fingers, and tapping the letter M twice on her palm for 'mother'. It was a clumsy effort to say that the kitten would die if not united with its mother, but Becky got the message. Her face filled with alarm, and she tugged at Jane's hand. Come, she signed, beckoning with her finger.

She led them to the great granite outcrop at the far end of the garden, the carn with its natural cave where children liked to play, and here they found Mitzi in a self-made nest of moss and last year's bracken suckling four kittens, all black like the last-born. When Jane laid the missing kitten beside her, Mitzi immediately began to wash it, and then the purring started—a deep, contented rumble.

Jane gave a resigned shake of her head. 'Carole went to such trouble to make Mitzi a bed in the wash-house, well out of reach of the children so that she wouldn't be disturbed—yet here she comes and has her kittens right in the place where most of the children who come here prefer to play. What shall we do?'

'Take Mitzi back to her rightful place and lock her in. Now she's got her kittens, she'll settle down. Will she claw me if I pick her up? She looks very fierce.'

'She's not fierce at all—she's actually very timid, and don't be put off by her claws—she only uses them on birds, trees and soft furnishings.'

Jane was proved right. Mitzi purred louder than ever when she was picked up, and rubbed her head against Scott's shoulder. 'I think she likes me,' Scott said, and Jane smiled.

'That's because she trusts you.'

The transfer to the wash-house was made quite easily,

Scott walking ahead with Mitzi, and Jane carrying the kittens, with Becky walking so close that she was almost leaning on her.

Mitzi took to the cat basket without any trouble. As Scott had said, she had asserted her independence, so now she was quite willing to fall in with their wishes. She washed all traces of Jane's touch from each kitten in turn, then settled down to suckle them with her engine running at full throttle.

Scott gave Jane a gentle nudge. 'Look at Becky,' he said. 'Listen!'

Becky's face was one huge beam of delight, and her eyes large and full of wonderment as she watched the kittens climbing over each other in their eager search for nourishment, their tiny paws treading in each other's eyes and noses, and their little pink mouths giving out silent mews. Above the rumbling of the mother cat, Jane heard another sound—a high-pitched note like a bat squeaking. Her mouth fell open.

'It's Becky!' she cried.

Scott nodded. 'I told you something like this could happen. It's only a beginning, but it's something you're going to hear a lot more of in future—and it's going to get stronger.'

Tears welled into Jane's eyes; she had to fight back an urge to pick Becky up and cover her face with kisses. This wasn't a time for emotion—this was a time for celebration. 'One way and another it's been quite an afternoon,' she laughed, blinking her tears away. 'What a lot we'll have to tell the others when they return!'

'I think it's best if we let them get over the shock of Mitzi first. Then we'll tell them about Becky. Perhaps by then we'll have something more to tell them,' said Scott hopefully. But there were no more squeaks from Becky. She was solemn now, a self-appointed guardian angel, squatting by the side of the cat basket. Jane could see big waves ahead when it came time to part her from them.

When, on her return, Carole was met with the news of

Mitzi's misdemeanour, she refused to believe it. 'You're having me on,' she said, looking from Scott to Jane, the last ones she would have suspected of playing a stupid joke on her. She gave a half-hearted laugh. 'It's something you've cooked up between you—it isn't true, is it?'

'Come along and see for yourself,' said Scott, and, taking her gently by her arm, he led her towards the stables. The others followed, Luke and Dinah exchanging puzzled looks, unsure whether to believe the story or not.

Even when Carole was shown the evidence, she still couldn't believe it. 'They can't be Mitzi's kittens! They're not even Siamese!'

'They're half-Siamese,' said Luke. For the first time in days, he was smiling with real humour and the smile lit up his face, erasing the lines of worry.

'How can they be *half*-Siamese? They're all black!' Carole wailed.

Both Scott and Luke roared. 'They must be half-Siamese—Mitzi's the mother!' Then Scott explained about superfecundation—the fertilisation of two or more ova by different males. 'I think it highly likely that Mitzi had already been fertilised by some stray tom before you sent her to be mated.'

'I don't remember seeing any black cats around here—there was a tabby we were always shooing away.'

'It didn't have to be black. I've known this sort of thing happen before—half-Siamese are always black, though sometimes they have a touch of white about them.'

'*Half*-Siamese!' said Carole scathingly. 'I didn't want half-Siamese—I wanted whole ones.' Then she laughed, realising the absurdity of such a remark. She went down on her knees beside the basket and gently rubbed Mitzi's ears, then stroked each kitten in turn. 'They are adorable, aren't they? And they must have inherited some of their mother's characteristics.' Mitzi prodded Carole's hand with her head, asking to be stroked again, and Carole smiled. 'Yes, you're feeling very proud of yourself, aren't you? And you needn't be—you're a disgrace to the Siamese Cat Society.'

'She's gone up in my estimation,' Luke said. 'I don't like pampered cats. I like a female who knows her own mind and does what she thinks is right, in spite of outside pressures.'

The others were amused at what they took as a rather pedantic defence of a cat, but Jane thought it was a dig at her. Luke didn't intend that, and he had a moment of remorse when he saw the colour run in and out of her cheeks, then thought, Well, if the hat fits, let her wear it!

Dinah looked troubled. 'You won't have them put down, will you?' she asked her mother. 'You won't have them destroyed because they're not pure pedigree?'

Carole was shocked and hurt at such a suggestion. 'What kind of a monster do you think I am?' she cried. 'Of course I won't have them put down—the very idea!'

'But you were going to sell them—you said it would more than make up the cost of the stud fee.'

Carole went pink. 'Honestly, Dinah, anyone hearing you would think I'm some kind of money-grubber. I don't need the money. All I shall be interested in later is finding good homes for the kittens.'

'Not all of them. Couldn't I keep one for myself?'

Now Carole was astonished. She stared at Dinah as if seeing her for the first time. Her eyes suddenly watered. 'You really would like a little kitten of your own? A pet? Oh, Dinah, that's a super idea—you can have the pick of the bunch.'

'Then I'll choose that one.' It was the one that Becky had purloined earlier, distinguishable from the others by a white tip to its tail. 'And I'm going to call it Tippy,' Dinah said. 'And don't anybody ask me why!'

'The next thing,' said Carole happily, 'is where do we keep them? I'm reluctant to leave them here, in case Mitzi takes it into her head to cart them all back to the carn. I'd rather have her in the house, as long as we can find somewhere where the children won't get at her.'

Scott interrupted. 'Forget about Mitzi for the moment. We've got something far more important to tell you. Jane and I heard Becky trying to laugh. It was when she was watching the kittens being fed—something must have amused her.'

In the stillness that followed Scott's remark, Mitzi's purrs sounded like the rumble of distant thunder.

'Are you sure?' Luke sounded sceptical. 'It couldn't have been the kittens you heard?'

'It was Becky,' said Scott with conviction.

Luke looked at Jane. 'And you heard her, too?' He looked like a man desperately wanting to believe, but fearful that such a belief could backfire on him.

'It was just a little squeak, but I heard it.'

Mitzi was forgotten. All eyes now turned on Becky, who hadn't moved from her place by the basket since Mitzi had been put there.

Luke sighed. 'Well, it's obvious she's not going to laugh to order—something will have to trigger it off again. Scott, if it's true, you know what it means, don't you? It will give us something to work on.' Luke closed his eyes like a man praying. When he spoke again his tone was brisker. 'We can't sit around here waiting for a miracle—Carole, you'd better do something about those kittens, and, Dinah, you should have a rest. You've had enough excitement for one day.'

Carole bent to pick up the cat basket, with the intention of carrying it and its occupants up to the house, but Becky had other ideas. Scarlet in the face with fury, and her eyes snapping like blue fire, she hung on to the basket as if her life depended upon it. It would have been a tug of war between them if Luke hadn't intervened. He picked Becky up, but it was just like trying to keep hold of an eel as she wriggled to get out of his grasp. Tears either of fear or frustration poured down her cheeks.

'Quickly,' he said over his shoulder to Carole. 'Get those damn cats out of sight—they're upsetting the child.'

Afterwards Scott gave what he considered the reason for Becky's sudden frenzy. 'She must have picked up the vibes between Dinah and her mother, and Dinah's fear that the kittens were to be done away with somehow transmitted itself to her, and when she saw Carole pick up the basket that's what she thought was going to happen to them.'

But he had no time for that explanation then, he was busy holding the door open for Carole as she and Dinah, both very subdued, struggled through with the basket between them. A sudden long-drawn-out cry of anguish followed them. Carole turned pale. 'That was Becky!' She made to turn back, but Scott stopped her.

'You two go on,' he said gently. 'Jane and I will stay with Luke. Go and put the kettle on—we'll need a cup of tea.'

'I think a stiff drink all round is more in order after the things that have happened this afternoon!' answered Carole, but she did as Scott said, continuing on her way with Dinah close beside her—closer than they had been in years.

After that one long painful cry, Becky went limp. No more struggling—no more flailing of arms and legs. Like a rag doll, she lay in Luke's arms, staring piteously up at him.

Jane saw the unmistakable glint of tears in Luke's eyes as he bent his head to give Becky a kiss. This was a moment of privacy for father and child, she thought, and she joined Scott at the door, too choked to say a word. They stood looking out over the sun-filled garden and beyond to the blue sparkling waters of the Atlantic.

'What now?' said Jane when she could trust herself to speak. 'What is the next move regarding Becky.'

'I don't really know, that's something I would like to discuss with Luke, but not now, perhaps later. Let's leave them on their own for a while. Come along, Jane—let's go in search of that cup of tea.'

CHAPTER NINE

MARIE'S reaction to the news about Mitzi was predictable. 'I wouldn't put anything past that pampered cross-eyed creature!' she stormed. 'A cat that turns up its nose at best liver and goes off and kills baby birds is capable of anything. And she needn't expect I'll save the top of the milk for her in future—water's good enough for her, the alley-cat!'

In spite of this indictment, it was Marie who found the ideal place for Mitzi and her kittens, in a little cubby-hole under the stairs next to the broom cupboard, handy enough to keep under observation, but well hidden from the children.

Marie was thrilled with the news about Becky—but not surprised. 'I knew it was only a matter of time,' she said. 'Dr Reevers said so.'

'I don't know how Scott does it,' Carole remarked to Jane later. 'Females find him irresistible—they all fall for him. Even Marie.'

'And Mitzi,' Jane added.

For the time being, Jane had forgotten her cares. Nobody could stay down-hearted in the atmosphere that prevailed in the old house that evening. There was hope abroad. Jane could see it in Carole's face when Dinah smiled at her, and in Scott's face when he looked at Carole, and in Luke's when he looked at little Becky. And for herself? Hope stopped there.

Scott and Luke had spent an hour before dinner discussing Becky's future. What steps to take now—which

135

treatment? Scott had been invited to stay and dine with them, and, though he protested that he couldn't keep accepting their hospitality, that he was having more meals with them than at his hotel, Luke retorted that they only wanted his company in order to pick his brains.

'It's good to see Luke his old cheerful self,' Carole remarked. 'He's been so quiet lately. It's good for him to have male company for a change—poor Luke, constantly surrounded by females.'

'This female is hungry. What's for dinner, Mummy?' Dinah put in at this point. 'Mummy' was an affectionate term she hadn't used for years. Carole told Jane this later, her eyes filling with happy tears.

Marie and Carole prepared dinner together that night while Jane put the children to bed. And an exuberant, noisy young group they were, too, not at all like the forlorn visitors who had arrived the day before. To Jane's surprise, Dinah asked if she could help.

Jane looked doubtful. 'I know you've had a rest this afternoon, but the children are so excited, you might find them a bit much. What did Luke say?'

'I didn't ask him. He's still closeted in the study with Scott—I expect they're on their second bottle of sherry by now.'

'You could supervise the children cleaning their teeth—particularly the little ones. That would be a big help.'

Jane was even more surprised to see how good Dinah was with the children. She had picked up enough sign language to make herself understood, and she was a dab hand at mime. A natural actress, Jane thought her, and told her so. But Dinah had other ideas.

'What do you have to do to become a nurse?' she asked when the children had finally settled down and she was helping Jane fold up their clothes, sorting out those that would need washing.

'For one thing, you would have to go back to school and get some good exam results——'

Dinah gave an exaggerated sigh. 'I knew there would be a catch in it!'

'Are you really interested in becoming a nurse, or is it just a passing fancy?' Jane was doubtful.

Dinah winked. 'Ask me that in a year's time,' she said.

'I won't be here then.'

'Want a bet on it? Only this afternoon I heard Mum say to Luke, "You mustn't let her go,"—meaning you, of course. "You must persuade her to stay, use some of your charm on her." Have you ever seen Luke using his charm, Jane?'

'Not lately,' said Jane, trying to be as flippant as Dinah, but feeling more like crying.

Becky was not ready for bed. She had fallen asleep on Luke's lap earlier, when they were having tea in the living-room, and he wouldn't let her be disturbed. Later, when she did wake, she stared about her in some confusion, but as awareness dawned she sat up and beamed at all the faces watching her. She seemed none the worse for her experiences of the afternoon—perhaps she was unaware of the cry she had uttered. She did remember the kittens, however, and even the bribe of a chocolate biscuit wouldn't keep her from seeing them—now! She signed the word, giving an emphatic drop of her flattened hand.

Once she had been shown that Mitzi and her kittens were safe, and it had been impressed upon her that their hiding-place was to be kept a secret, she was quite content. The thought of sharing a secret with the grown-ups gave her enormous satisfaction, but when she was allowed to hold one of the kittens her cup of happiness brimmed over. She put it gently to her lips and kissed it before handing it back to Jane, then she trotted back to the living-room and asked for her chocolate biscuit.

Jane had to prise her from the television when it was finally time for her to go to bed. Becky had her supper with Marie, making the most of being allowed to stay up. Jane had left the dining-table early, glad of the excuse that she had Becky to see to. The events of the day were beginning to make themselves felt, and she had the beginning of a headache. She longed for a chance to be on her own in order to sort out her thoughts. There had barely been time to take in Scott's story about Roger Barford before the episode with Mitzi had exploded upon her. Since then, she hadn't had a moment to herself.

The normally biddable Becky played up that night. Jane suspected she had had so much attention, she was reluctant to let it end. She looked like an angel in her white nightie, but she certainly didn't behave like one. She wouldn't let Jane leave her, signing that she wanted Jane to read to her, her lovely eyes so beseeching that Jane's heart melted.

Becky was quite capable of reading to herself, but she liked Jane to show her picture books—especially some battered copies of old-time favourites like *Cinderella* and *Beauty and the Beast* that used to belong to Dinah. Any book with an illustration of a princess or a bride in it appealed to Becky. When Jane stumbled over a word, or had forgotten the sign language of a particular passage, Becky happily helped her out. Tonight, between them, they worked their way through *The Sleeping Beauty*, *Little Red Riding Hood* and *Snow White* before Jane called a halt. Becky protested at first, but soon gave in when Jane rubbed her head and grimaced with pain, for she understood that. When Jane wished her goodnight she pulled her hands from under the covers and signed goodnight in return. Jane drew the curtains and switched on the night-light beside the bed. All the dormitories had night-lights—if any of the children needed something during the night, they wouldn't be able to explain in the dark.

Jane had to pass Luke's study on the way to her bedroom. Noticing that his door was ajar, she trod lightly, her footsteps making no sound on the thick carpet, but Luke either sensed her or saw her. He opened the door. 'Would you come in a moment?' he said.

Jane drew back. Nothing—nothing would induce her to enter that room again, she told herself. 'I—I've got a bad head—I was just going to lie down for a few minutes.' Her excuse, though genuine, sounded lame.

'I won't keep you.' Luke opened the door wider, and it seemed childish not to comply.

As she entered the room Jane saw that he had been writing letters. His desk-top was strewn with papers, and there was a partly typed sheet of paper in the typewriter. He was dealing with the correspondence that she would have been doing but for the rift between them.

'Sit down,' he said.

'I can't stay——'

'Sit down, please.' The please sounded more like an order than a request, and Jane did as she was told, taking a chair as far from him as possible.

It didn't make it any easier for her that he didn't sit himself, but prowled about the room in a restless manner. Once he went towards the other desk—the roll-top desk in the window recess—and she had the uncomfortable feeling that he was going to produce something that would invariably lead to the subject of her deception. She gripped her hands together—she couldn't go all through that again—but he had only gone to straighten one of the drawers that had been pushed in crookedly. He returned and looked at her under his brows, and she felt the full impact of his blue gaze.

Unexpectedly, his next words were, 'I wanted to thank you for all the help you've given today. I'm afraid with the excitement over Mitzi—and more so with Becky, though that wasn't exactly excitement—if it hadn't been for you our little visitors would have been neglected. I must say I was very impressed by the way you stepped in and took over.'

It was an overture of friendship, there was no doubt about that, but there was something lacking. He was still a man under restraint; he still couldn't bring himself to show any real warmth towards her. Because of her nagging head, because her nerves were taut, because she could never be her natural self with him, she didn't stop to think, but blurted out, 'Did Carole put you up to this?'

At first he didn't understand. 'Did Carole put me up to what?' Then angry colour suffused his cheeks. He said curtly, 'Do you think I haven't a mind of my own?'

'I know only too well that you have a mind of your own. And once you've made up your mind about something, you don't change it, do you?' Jane was near to tears. She hadn't wanted this to happen—this silly squabble. She welcomed his offer of friendship, lukewarm though it was, but thoughtlessly had flung it back at him. Was it too late to try again?

'I'm only doing what I'm being paid to do,' she said conciliatorily, but that wasn't the right thing to say, either, because she saw Luke wince. She added quickly, 'I haven't done any more than Marie—she's been on the go all day.'

'But we're not talking about Marie, we're talking about you,' he said stiffly. 'I particularly wanted to thank you for the way you've coped with Dinah. I've seen a great improvement in her—you're a good influence.'

She stared at him in outrage, speechless.

He raised his eyebrows. 'Why do you look at me like that?'

All the pent-up feelings of the past week came pouring out of her then. '*You* can say that I'm a good influence on Dinah? A *good* influence, when you think of me as untrustworthy, lacking in dignity and integrity, dishonest——'

'When did I say that?'

'Not in so many words, perhaps, but you implied it—in this very room—last Sunday!'

His face went taut with strain. 'I don't remember exactly what I said then, though I do remember how disappointed I felt in you. But afterwards, when I thought over what you'd told me about your nephew——' He hesitated. 'What you did was wrong, but you did it for the right reasons, and last night, at the Garrison, I hoped——' He stopped himself impatiently. 'Then you let slip the name of the man you'd been working for—the man who'd sent you here to spy on me—Roy Barford. Just another deception, I thought, but I don't care any more. My feelings—your feelings, they're nothing compared with what's happened here today. Becky used her voice for the first time. That was a miracle—a very small, insignificant miracle, but a miracle all the same. It won't cure her deafness—she won't be able to hear, but *we'll* be able to hear her—we'll hear her laugh, and we'll hear her cry. Surely that will add another dimension to her life?'

His impassioned words brought a constriction to Jane's throat. She swallowed, not trusting herself with words—not trusting herself to meet the eyes of the man who looked so careworn and exultant at the same time.

'I'm offering you an olive-branch, Jane,' he said quietly. 'For the short time left to you here, couldn't we work together without recriminations? It will make it so much easier for us both. And now, before you get in first and accuse me of having an ulterior motive—yes, I admit that I have. Scott has told me of a speech therapist—retired now, but who, for years prior to his retirement, worked with deaf children. He thinks that if anybody can help Becky, he can. The man lives near Buckingham, and Scott is going to ring him from his hotel tomorrow. If this Mr Arnold is agreeable, I'll take Becky to see him. It might mean I'll be away for a few days, so you can see why it's more important than ever that you stay on. You'll be needed far more now.'

It was an olive-branch with thorns attached. He wanted her to stay because she was useful to him—there was nothing more in it than that. But at least he was being honest with her—he wasn't pretending. She knew that if he could do without her, he would, as she was becoming an embarrassment to him—a reminder of things he would rather forget. That was why she had to make him see that she hadn't known about Roger Barford.

'I know you haven't got a very high opinion of me,' she said. 'But I'm not as bad as you think. I had no idea of your connection with Roger Barford until this afternoon when Dr Reevers told me. I knew nothing about Roger Barford—I'd never heard his name before this afternoon. I didn't even know Roy had a younger brother, and that's the honest truth!'

Her denials faded away into a whisper—it was useless to keep on protesting. She could see that Luke didn't believe her. He wanted to, she could see that, too, by the glimmer of hope that crossed his face, but it soon gave way to doubt.

'How long were you working for Roy Barford?' he asked quietly.

'Just over two years.'

'And in all that time you never discovered that he had a brother? Nobody on the staff mentioned it to you?'

'We weren't a large staff,' she protested. 'The *Moonraker* was a small, weekly paper—little more than a gossip-sheet—we doubled up on different jobs and we all worked hard. We didn't have time to talk or speculate about the boss. The older ones might have known about his private life, but I didn't—for the simple reason that I wasn't interested!'

He smiled—a smile that didn't reach his eyes. 'Let's leave

it there, shall we, or this argument will go on all evening. We've agreed to bury the hatchet. Let's forget everything else and carry on from there——'

'I can't carry on from there, whatever that means!' she shouted as her control finally snapped. 'I'm tired of being disbelieved—of being put up with under sufferance. I've got my pride, too. I resent being patronised, and I'm sick of being treated as a cheat and liar. Oh, I'll stay—you needn't fear I won't. I'll stay on because the children need me, not because you want me to. I don't care a fig what you think any longer. All I know is that I want to finish my time here and then get away as quickly as possible. And then I hope I never see you again!'

Jane didn't know how she got out of the room after that. Later, she remembered blundering along the corridor and into her room and bolting the door, then flinging herself face down on the bed. She couldn't cry, though tears would have helped. A rapid, rhythmic beat pounded in her ears, and she listened for some time before realising it was the sound of her heart.

Never before had she lost control of herself like that, and she was ashamed of the passion she had unleashed. She shivered, yet she wasn't cold; her face burned.

She had the impression that Luke had called after her, but she couldn't be sure. His image came before her—the handsome dark head, the fearless blue eyes. She loved him—only now in the aftermath of remorse could she see how much she loved him, and she had told him she couldn't bear the sight of him! It was the biggest lie she had told yet.

She rolled over on her back, kicking off her shoes as she did so, lifting her legs on to the bed. Her limbs felt like lead, yet she had the sensation that she was floating—hovering near the ceiling, looking down at the exhausted, dry-eyed girl on the bed.

Daylight was fading when she woke. She sat up and

stared around her, too disorientated at first to remember if
it was morning or night. Realisation came swiftly, and with
it a feeling of anticlimax. What a fool she had made of
herself—and now she would have to get up and face Luke
again. She felt like shutting herself in her room until the
morning, but common sense told her that, if something
unpleasant had to be faced, it was better sooner than later.
She washed her face and brushed out her hair, and replaced
her crumpled dress with her shaggy sweater and jeans.

The upper hall light was on, and also the light at the head
of the stairs. She descended cautiously, listening for sounds.
Everywhere was so quiet, she was sure the house was
empty. Voices were coming from the kitchen—a man and
woman arguing. She stopped and listened, and realised it
was the television—Marie was viewing. She went on to the
living-room, which was empty—so was the dining-room.
The cloth had been cleared and a big bowl of anemones had
been replaced in the centre of the table.

She had heard Carole tell Scott she would drive him back
to Hugh Town after dinner, so presumably Luke and
Dinah had gone with them. Jane felt she had had a reprieve
for the time being, yet she couldn't relax. How could she
fill in the time until they returned? Not with
Marie—nothing escaped Marie's sharp eyes. Not even
hidden tension.

The garden called her. Jane stood at the open front door,
took in several deep breaths of salt sea air, and felt better for
it. Her headache was gone, but it had left her feeling dull
and listless. A turn in the garden would do her good.

The air was moist and scented with the fragrance of
wallflowers. A tender breeze gently rustled the leaves of the
palm trees. A night for lovers, thought Jane wistfully. A
night for love—all soft shadows and sweet smells.

She wandered to the end of the drive and back again, then
round to the side of the house and saw a patch of light

outlined on the grass. It was coming from one of the upper windows, and, looking up, Jane saw through the undrawn curtains the shadow of a man. Luke hadn't gone out—he was in his study working.

Jane retraced her steps, heading back towards the front of the house. The noise of a vehicle lumbering up the lane drowned the twitterings of the roosting birds, and she recognised the sound of the minibus. She went down to meet it, and Carole alighted on her own.

She peered at Jane, trying to read her face in the gathering dusk. 'How are you feeling now? Luke said you had a headache, so we wouldn't disturb you. It's a wonder we haven't all lost the tops of our heads, after all we've been through today. It's been a wonderful day, though, hasn't it?' She finished on a deep, contented sigh.

'Dinah isn't with you?'

'She wanted to come, but Luke decided she had had enough excitement for one day and sent her to bed.' Carole slipped her arm through Jane's. 'It's too good to go in. Walk with me round the garden. I'll leave the bus for Luke to put away.'

They walked in companionable silence. Where the shadows were deeper, the scent of flowers seemed stronger—the scent of bluebells and lilac that grew in a wild part of the garden. Small white moths the size of snowflakes fluttered about them.

Carole broke the silence. 'Scott is returning to London on Wednesday. He's asked me if I'll bring Dinah to spend a weekend with him at his flat soon. He's hoping to arrange for David, his son, to take a weekend away from school at the same time. He wants us to meet him.'

'How did Dinah take that?'

Carole chuckled. 'Would you believe, she liked the idea? She said she always wanted an older brother—and she said it in front of Scott, too—deliberately. I could have crowned her!'

'Could you really, Carole?'

'No, of course not.' Carole squeezed Jane's arm. 'Of all the nicest things that have come out of this past week, it's the better relationship between Dinah and me. I really feel that in future we're going to be good friends, and I don't know how it happened.'

'Illness changes people,' said Jane wisely. 'Sometimes for the worse, but more often for the better. It seems to make them more understanding of others—more appreciative. Dinah was only really ill for forty-eight hours, but you never left her side in all that time. That proved to her that you really loved her—and that's all she needed.'

'Take a little—give a little,' said Carole happily. 'I shall be more tolerant in future, not make so much fuss when she does something I don't approve of. Parents are inclined to think they own their children, and I'm no exception.' Carole suddenly noticed the light in Luke's study. 'Poor Luke, he's still working—he's always at it.' She became thoughtful, and said, 'Jane, do you remember the day you arrived you said something about Becky being one of the family, and I took umbrage and was rude to you?'

'You weren't rude—mildly reproving me for not minding my own business, that's all.' Jane spoke lightly, though her heart had begun to race at Carole's words. She hoped the subject would not be pursued, but it was.

'I was ashamed for the way I turned on you,' Carole said. 'After all, it was an obvious mistake to make—there *is* a family likeness. It's a touchy subject with me, I'm afraid,' she added apologetically. 'I couldn't understand why Luke wouldn't be open with me about Becky—wouldn't tell me anything about her earlier life. All I knew was that she'd been living with Robin and Luke in Tuscany. Poor Robin only lived another year after Luke joined him. Luke stayed on for another three years, winding up the estate. Three years seems an awful long time to me to wind up anybody's affairs. I think Luke had another reason for staying away from England—perhaps because of his health. It had certainly improved by the time he got back home again. His job had been getting him down—four years away from all that pressure had worked wonders for him.'

Carole paused. She stared at the western sky, where a sickle-shaped moon glimmered behind thin cloud. 'The only thing I knew for certain about Becky was that she was deaf and had been neglected as a baby, which made her backward for her age—not mentally, she's bright enough, but in other ways. She's more like a four-year-old the way she ties those soft toys together, don't you think?'

'There could be a psychological reason for that,' Jane said.

'I know. Don't think I'm criticising Becky; I'm not. I've become very, very fond of her, but I can't help comparing her with Dinah when she was that age—but then Dinah was rather a precocious little madam.' Carole drew in her breath on a sudden sigh. 'Do you see any likeness between Dinah and Becky, Jane?'

'Not a scrap. Why?'

'Because I feel that Ned could have been Becky's father.'

Jane was taken aback at this. 'Whatever grounds have you got for thinking that?' she asked.

'Only Luke's reluctance to tell me who the parents are. Why else would he be so cagey about her, if not to spare me pain?' Carole gave an edgy little laugh. 'I may be doing poor Ned an injustice, but he had the opportunity. He was away on business a lot, making extended trips to Europe, and he attracted the ladies—I used to tease him about it. But we had such a good relationship, I always felt that if he had strayed off the straight and narrow he would have told me about it. Perhaps he intended to, but died before he got the chance.'

'I don't think your husband was Becky's father,' said Jane slowly. 'I believe Luke is.'

Carole wasn't surprised at this statement. 'That crossed my mind, too, but why should he keep it a secret? Luke has nothing to hide—he's not married, there's no serious attachment to anyone. I think if Becky was his daughter, he'd shout it from the rooftops!'

Jane thought back to the last time she and Luke had really been close, having coffee together in the restaurant overlooking the harbour. Luke had been talking about Becky, and he had used the term 'Becky's natural father', and she had assumed he had been referring to himself. Could he have meant Robin?

She said aloud, 'Have you considered Robin?'

'Robin?' Carole's voice always softened when she spoke of Robin. 'No. Robin couldn't have been Becky's father—I think he was too sick to father a child. In any case, there was only ever one woman for him, and I couldn't imagine her having a baby. It might have spoiled her figure!'

Jane smiled. 'Having a baby didn't spoil your figure.'

'You didn't know Kirsty Brownlow. She wasn't the sort to give up nearly a year of her life bearing a child—it might have interfered with her career.'

'Kirsty Brownlow?' Jane repeated stupidly, remembering the photo of the girl in Luke's desk—the letter she had posted for him.

'Perhaps you don't remember her. She was a pop star, very successful about ten years ago—perhaps more successful in America than she was over here. Robin met her at a party, and immediately became besotted with her. He was a brilliant pianist—on his way to becoming a virtuoso, but he threw all that up in order to become Kirsty's accompanist. Later, when she formed a group, he became their manager. Believe me, Jane, that girl was only interested in one thing—Kirsty Brownlow. She didn't love Robin, but she needed him. He had a flair for promotion and management, and she exploited that.'

They had encircled the shrubbery and were heading back to the house. The scent of the wallflowers hung like a pall of fragrance embracing the shadows. For the rest of her life, whenever Jane smelled wallflowers, she remembered that night.

'Shall I finish telling you about Robin, or are you tired of hearing my voice?' Carole asked.

Knowing more about Robin could mean understanding Luke better. 'You can't stop now,' Jane said.

'Ned and Luke were very bitter about the way Robin had sacrificed himself for this girl. I didn't see it as a sacrifice. Loving Kirsty, serving her, meant more to Robin than becoming a concert pianist. I understood that, and after a while Ned came to accept it, too. But Luke never did. He had a blazing row with Robin—in front of Kirsty, too, and she never forgave him. She saw to it that the two brothers never came together again after that—not while she had Robin in her grip, anyway. I think that was the reason Luke threw up his career with the Home Office—to be with Robin when he was dying. He was trying to make up for those lost years.'

'What happened to this Kirsty Brownlow?'

'With Robin's help she had become a very rich woman. They toured the world—the money rolled in. Robin invested his, and also bought a villa in Tuscany, and when he became too ill to work any longer he went off to live there. He begged Kirsty to go with him—to marry him. But she wouldn't give up her career.

'The group carried on for a while, but without Robin they weren't the same. Something in their performance was lacking, and their popularity began to wane, so they decided to split up. Kirsty carried on on her own with another manager, but never achieved the success she did with Robin. The last I heard of her she was singing in a nightclub in Vancouver.'

They entered the house by a side door. Carole paused on the step. 'By the way, Jane, don't mention Kirsty Brownlow to Luke. Don't let him know I told you anything about her. Luke hasn't seen or heard of her in years, and I wouldn't want to be responsible for opening old wounds.'

Jane gave her promise readily, knowing how easy it would be to keep, but she did wonder why Carole thought Luke had not been in touch with Kirsty Brownlow for years. The letter Jane had posted seemed to point otherwise.

CHAPTER TEN

SCOTT phoned on Monday morning to say that he had been in touch with Mr Arnold, or rather his wife, as Mr Arnold was out. She said her husband would be in soon after midday, and would Luke call then? Luke sought out Carole to tell her this, and found her with Jane in the playroom, supervising the children writing cards to send to their parents to say they had arrived safely—a duty that had been postponed from the day before.

This was the first time Jane had come face to face with Luke since the scene in his study. He had stayed up late working until long after the others had gone to bed, then had risen early to go for a walk before breakfast, and Jane had had hers before he returned.

His manner now was so natural that he was either putting on an act in front of Carole, or perhaps was so cheered up at the thought of something being done for Becky that the contretemps between them faded in importance. More than likely, Jane thought sorrowfully, it was of no significance to him.

'How are you going to contain yourself until midday?' asked Carole. 'I can see you're bursting with impatience already.'

'I'm going down to see Scott. I've got a proposition to put to him. If this Arnold is willing to see Becky straight away, I'll take her tomorrow. If I can't get seats in the helicopter, I'll charter a light plane. Then I intend to hire a car from a garage in Penzance. I don't say driving all that way would be quicker than going by rail, but it would be easier—for

150

Becky, anyway—and a darn sight more convenient. If Scott is willing to shorten his holiday by one day, he could come with me and we'd share the driving. He can go from Buckingham to London by train; it's not a long journey. Have you any objection, Carole?'

'What's it got to do with me?' said Carole, trying not to look smug.

'I thought you might have planned one last romantic evening together,' Luke teased. 'Well, I'm off—see you later.'

Carole called after him. 'Just a minute, Luke—Jane is going into town to do some shopping for us. If you could give her a lift, it would save her waiting for the bus——'

Jane felt a tremor go through her. 'But I don't mind waiting for the bus,' she broke in hastily. 'And there are still some more cards to do yet——'

'Only a few, and I can finish those off.'

'Perhaps Jane prefers to go by bus,' Luke said quietly.

Carole was particularly obtuse that morning. She didn't notice Jane's embarrassment or Luke's indifference. 'What's the point of Jane waiting another half-hour for the bus when she could go with you now?' she said maddeningly, and there was no answer to that.

'I'm sorry you've been let in for this,' Luke apologised once they were outside the room. 'It can't be easy for you to accept a favour from someone you dislike.'

'I don't dislike you.' Jane turned quickly away, and her words were almost lost.

'You gave a very good impression of it last night.' Luke's laugh was hollow. He could just see the reddened curve of Jane's cheek and her trembling mouth. She reminded him of a fearful child, and his antagonism faded. 'Cheer up, Jane,' he said kindly. 'You won't have to put up with me for much longer.

His kindness was nearly Jane's undoing. She felt the

tears gathering at the backs of her eyes. He had called her Jane, something he hadn't done in days. But he could afford to be friendly now—he, too, hadn't to put up with her for much longer. The thought filled her with despair, but she had to go on with the pretence—to protect that unstable, disturbing symbol she called her pride.

It was quite an effort to turn and face him, to say what had to be said. 'I wish to apologise for last night—I said things I didn't mean. It was very stupid of me to lose control like that. I'm sorry.' She was very proud of herself. Her voice hadn't once quivered, and she had held his gaze. It was a magnificent pose of impassiveness.

Luke looked tired. She saw him sigh, and he ran his fingers through his hair, which in anyone else she would have seen as a nervous gesture. Suddenly he straighted his shoulders, as if jerking himself out of apathy, and gave her a faint smile. '*Pax*, is it, then?' he said, reverting to a word from his childhood. 'Let's shake on it, shall we?'

He held out his hand and, after only a slight hesitation, Jane complied. His fingers closed over hers, a firm, sure grip, and at his touch a surge of longing went through her. No, it was more than longing, it was a need of him—the need of his arms around her, to hear his deep voice murmuring tender words of love. This is what it could have been like from the beginning, she thought, then reality took over, and stiffly she withdrew her hand.

'What's all this?' Dinah was coming down the stairs, smiling as if something amused her. She looked knowingly from one to the other of them. 'Have you two got some secret pact?'

'We don't have any secrets, do we, Jane?' said Luke, but not looking at her. He seemed to welcome Dinah's intervention. His manner changed, became hearty. 'Well, young Dinah, how do you feel after yesterday's activity? Strong enough to come with Jane and me to Hugh Town?'

He'd rather risk Dinah's health than be alone with me, Jane thought unfairly. Dinah herself looked surprised. 'Do you think I'm up to it?' she asked.

'Providing you don't tire yourself, and Jane will see to it that you don't. I'll drop you off at the Square. Jane has to do some shopping, but I'm meeting Scott. You can come along with me if you like?'

'What? To listen to you talking more shop? No, thank you.'

Jane was glad of Dinah's company in the minibus—it prevented awkward silences. There was no lack of energy where Dinah's tongue was concerned! When they alighted she asked Luke whether he was taking them home again, or should they catch the bus?

Luke took a note from his wallet. 'If I'm not here by half-past eleven, take a taxi,' he said. 'I may be held up—you know what it's like when I get talking to Scott. Take care of yourselves, girls, and don't buy up all the shops.'

He drove on, turning up the hill to the hotel where Scott was staying. Dinah looked at note he had given her, folded it and tucked it in her purse. 'Do you think he'll mind if we treat ourselves to coffee out of it?'

'I can treat you to coffee.'

'Let Luke—he's got oodles of money.'

Jane insisted that Dinah waited for her in the park instead of trailing around the town, and found her a seat near a bright clump of hydrangeas. 'You make me feel like an oldie—only OAPs come and sit in here,' Dinah protested, but when Jane returned weighed down by two bulging shopping bags, it wasn't pensioners she found sharing the seat with Dinah, it was three tall, presentable, fair-haired young men.

'I can't leave you a minute,' said Jane, dragging the reluctant Dinah away. 'Three of them—all chatting you up!'

'They weren't chatting me up, they were practicing their English. They come from Denmark.'

'Danes don't have to practice their English, they all speak it fluently,' retorted Jane, but she smiled. Dinah was flushed with pleasure—nobody looking at her would dream she was suffering from glandular fever.

There were not only Danes in the town, there were Germans and French, too. The Scillies were a popular holiday resort with Europeans, many of them sailing over in their own boats.

Jane cast an eye skyward—there were ominous signs of rain, and the wind had freshened. Neither of the girls had brought jackets with them, and Dinah in her sleeveless top was shivering.

'What say we skip coffee in town and have it with Marie?' Jane suggested, adding as bait, 'She made a fresh batch of drop scones this morning.'

They were back at Nightingale House in less than half an hour. Luke followed them in by a few minutes. He went straight up to his study and put through the long awaited call to Mr Arnold. Later, Jane heard the outcome of the call from Carole.

'Well,' Carole said, 'Luke and Mr Arnold hit it off very well; I think that's a good sign. Luke said Frank Arnold has one of those voices that inspires confidence. Anyway, he said he could see Becky any time, and when Luke suggested tomorrow he agreed. Scott is going with them. Luke says the Arnolds are running some kind of a smallholding—Mr Arnold's dream, he said, for his retirement. At present they have two small grandsons staying with them. Luke could hear them in the background making a terrible din, and a dog barking—sounded like a bit of a menagerie, he said.'

'That should please Becky.'

'Yes, you're right. Anyway, what all this is leading up to, Jane, is—do you mind putting the children to bed on your own again? Tonight, I mean. Scott has asked me to dine with him—for the very last time this holiday, he said.'

'Perhaps Dinah will help me out, then?'

'Sorry, Jane, but Scott wants Dinah to come along, too. I do feel awful about it.'

'Nonsense. Take the opportunity while you can, you might not see him again for weeks.'

Jane successfully hid from Carole her dread that, once the children were in bed, the evening might prove to be a repeat performance of the evening before. She felt she couldn't take the risk of being alone with Luke again, but she worried unduly, as he decided not to come down to supper. He told Marie he had some important work to clear up before heading east in the morning, and would she take him up something light on a tray?

Jane watched as Marie set out a tray with ham and salad, rolls, butter and cheese. 'Would you like me to take that upstairs for you?' she felt obliged to ask, praying inwardly for Marie to refuse, which she did.

'No, you stay there and take the weight off your feet. You look really knocked-up tonight. Those kids take it out of you; I can see that. I'll just nip this up to Dr Springer, then I'll get us something tasty for supper.'

There was something simmering on the stove that gave out a pungent fishy smell—so overpowering that it drove Jane to the window for some fresh air. The awful thought occurred to her that it might be the 'something tasty' Marie had planned for their supper.

Marie returned. 'I'll give Mitzi hers first, then we'll have ours,' she said complacently, and Jane watched open-mouthed as she strained the liquid from the smelly mess in the saucepan that turned out to be some greyish-white fish, which she carefully boned.

Jane was astounded. 'You're going to all that trouble for Mitzi? I thought you didn't like her.'

'I wouldn't let my worst enemy starve if she had a family to feed,' said Marie unctuously. 'Mitzi is partial to coley, and this is a nice bit of coley, though I don't fancy it myself. There, I can hear her miaowing outside the door, she must have smelled it.' Everybody could, Jane thought—the smell must have gone all over the house.

When Mitzi had been fed, and the kittens inspected, Marie was ready to serve supper. She took a lasagne out of the oven, all crispy and brown on top. Jane's mouth began to water.

'I have never tasted lasagne as good as this before,' she said after a few mouthfuls.

'That's because I'm not mean with the mince. I don't think much of a lasagne when you have to look for the meat with a magnifying glass. Have some more, Miss—er—yes?'

'Jane. Just once,' said Jane pleadingly.

'Jane, then,' said Marie, speaking as if she had a bone in her throat.

At half-past eight that evening, Jane put on her raincoat and tied a scarf over her head. She was going to the phone-box to call Roy at his flat in the Barbican. She had to find out why he hadn't been in touch—she was going to ask him about his brother. It was something she had been meaning to do since Scott's revelation. She knew she wouldn't have any rest until she heard the full story from Roy himself. Also, she wanted to go to Luke afterwards and tell him what she had done, hoping that might convince him that she had been speaking the truth when she had said she knew nothing about Roger Barford.

She was nearing the front door when Luke appeared on the stairs. He was carrying the tray, taking it back to the kitchen.

'Going out?' he said, looking surprised.

'Just to the phone.'

His eyes narrowed. She could sense his suspicion—it was

like something alive.

'What's the matter with this one?'

'Nothing. I don't want you to think I'm taking advantage.'

'I'm sure no one begrudges you a call. If you want to salve your conscience, put something in the phone-box.'

Jane realised she had backed herself into a corner. 'Actually, I was going to reverse the charges——'

Luke's face hardened. He had guessed to whom she was making her call. 'Then the question of cost doesn't arise, does it?' he said crisply.

'I've got nothing to hide,' Jane blurted out. 'I'm going to call Roy Barford—I'm going to challenge him about his brother. I'm going to ask him why he kept me in ignorance of him.'

Luke nodded to the phone on the hall-table. 'Then be my guest.'

But Jane wanted to be on her own when she phoned Roy. She had several things she wanted to straighten out with him, and she couldn't do it with Luke standing there, listening.

'I don't mind the walk to the phone-box—I quite like it,' she said lamely.

Luke gave a ghost of a smile. 'With the rain lashing down like this? Go on—use that phone. If you're worrying about me eavesdropping, don't. I'm going off to have a word with Marie.'

'No—stop!' Her cry rang after him. 'I don't mind you listening to what I have to say. I have nothing to hide!'

Nonchalantly, he balanced his tray on one hand. 'OK. Go ahead.'

Jane fumbled with the dial, finally got through to the operator, and asked for Roy's number. There seemed some delay, then the operator came back to her. 'I'm sorry, caller,' he said, 'but that number isn't answering.'

Jane replaced the receiver. 'There's no answer—Roy must be out,' she said.

'Just as well that you didn't go up to the phone-box, you would have got wet through for nothing. Cheer up. You can try again, later.' His apparent unconcern rattled her.

'I'd like to make another call,' she said. 'To my brother-in-law—to ask if there's any news of Jamie.'

Luke's expression softened. 'Of course. And this time, please, no nonsense about reversing the call. This one's on me.'

He waited to see if she took up the offer, then, satisfied, went on his way. Jane got through almost immediately, and Jim's answering hello was as clear as if he were in the same room.

'Jim, I'm so anxious to hear—any news?'

Jim sounded much happier than he had the last time she had spoken to him. 'Jane! I've been trying to get on to you, but the number was engaged. I had a call from Susan just a half-hour ago—midday there. She was very cheerful—Jamie is over his chest infection. Erik Tollesbury is hoping to operate as soon as he can fit Jamie into his list—could be this week, could be next. Susan has promised to phone as soon as she has any news. Remember us in your prayers, Jane.'

'I always do. Goodbye, Jim, and God bless.' Jane blinked away the welling tears. As a rule, she rarely cried, but just lately she seemed to be doing nothing else. Her emotions were on the surface, always ready to betray her.

The leave-taking with little Becky the following morning was another emotional occasion. The child was excited at the prospect of going off on an adventure with Luke, but at the same time bewildered by the fuss being made of her, and also somewhat anxious, as she wasn't sure what was awaiting her at the end of the journey.

Everybody gave her a going-away present. Sweets and

fruit from Carole, Marie and Dinah, a gift-box of soap and
talc from Jane, even some coloured shells from the hoard
collected by the children on Sunday. Becky accepted them
with the dignity of a queen receiving tributes from her
subjects. At the last minute, Jane thought of something else
and flew indoors to get it: the knitted kangaroo with the toy
giraffe in its pouch. Becky gave her a pitying look and shook
her head when it was offered to her.

'I think,' said Luke, not attempting to hide his
amusement, 'she's trying to tell you that she's above that
sort of thing now. How do you expect stuffed toys to
compete with live kittens?' But, to be on the safe side, Luke
took the kangaroo and stuffed it in the top of his holdall.

Scott arrived in the taxi that was to take them to the
airport. While he was saying his goodbyes to the others,
Jane managed to have a few minutes alone with Becky.

'I love you,' she said, signing in the words little Whitey
had taught her. Now, at this moment of parting, a dreadful
uncertainty took hold of Jane—the possibility that she
might never see Becky again. She swept the child into her
arms and clung to her, overcome by the strength of her
fears. In some strange, illogical way Becky and Jamie had
fused as one in her thoughts, each meaning as much to her
as the other.

There was a light touch on her shoulder. It was Luke.
'May I have Becky back again now?' he quipped. Looking
closer, he saw that Jane's deep brown eyes were
suspiciously moist. 'I didn't realise Becky meant so much to
you,' he said. 'I warned you when you first arrived not to
become too involved—you wouldn't be here long enough
for a permanent relationship.'

Does he keep reminding me of that on purpose? Jane
thought. She looked up and met his gaze—it was
thoughtful, even concerned. No, he hadn't meant his words
unkindly—he was just stating a fact.

'I think of her as I think of Jamie—both victims of circumstances, both so vulnerable——' She couldn't go on.

'What news of your nephew?'

'He may be operated on soon. I'm counting the days now, until I hear.'

Luke took a step nearer and squeezed her arm sympathetically. That gesture nearly cost Jane her pride—she was ready to throw herself into his arms—but a call from Scott saved her. He was pointing meaningfully at his watch—it was time to go.

Luke said, 'I'm leaving you in charge here, I know I can trust you. Just see that the children have a good time—that's the important thing.'

'I trust you'—a figure of speech only, nothing more significant than that, she told herself as she stood with the others and watched as the taxi drove off. Carole slipped her arm through Jane's in her usual manner. 'Now let's have that second cup of coffee before we make a start,' she said.

The rest of the day was an anticlimax—a time of waiting for the call Luke had promised to make. It came just after supper, when they were all in the kitchen clearing away the dishes. Carole went off to answer it. She was a long time away, and when she returned she was smiling.

'Dr Springer arrived safely, then?' said Marie.

'Actually, that was Scott calling.' No wonder Carole looked so pleased with herself. 'Yes, they had a good journey, and found Mr Arnold's place without any difficulty. Scott says it's in a picture-postcard village, and the Arnolds live in a picture-postcard house with plum trees growing against the wall. They have several acres of land put down to grass and vegetables and also some livestock—goats, ducks, hens, geese, that kind of thing. Oh, and a donkey who has just given birth to a foal. Becky is absolutely in her glory.'

'Is Becky staying with the Arnolds?' Jane asked.

'Yes, they insisted upon it, and had a room all ready for her. I gather she's already made friends with the two boys, and they all get on well together. The first thing the boys did was to show her their pet rabbits——'

'I bet she brings one back with her,' Dinah put in.

Carole folded the tablecloth and put it away in one of the drawers of the dresser. 'Mrs Arnold wanted Luke to stay with them, too. She said there was another spare room, but Luke felt it was better if he kept out of the way and left Becky with Mr Arnold. There's a hotel in the village, and he's booked in there. He left a message with Scott to say he'll phone here as soon as he's got any further news—but not to expect a letter, he'll be too busy. Apparently he has some business to see to in London.'

Remembering Luke's last words to her, about making sure that the children enjoyed themselves, Jane made a mental list of all the outings she could arrange for their benefit. Without Luke there would be no trips to the off-islands, but there was still plenty to see on St Mary's. Fine days, of course, would be spent on the beach, and there were many to choose from. Days not so fine could be spent in other pursuits. There were several places to visit—a museum, a glass-factory, pottery and woodwork shop—all instructive to the children, as well as full of interest. There were organised tours to the bulb fields to see how the industry had developed, and to a Heritage Centre. So much to see, in fact, they might not be able to get it all in. In the evenings, and it was light enough to keep the children up until late, there were slide and film shows on different aspects of life in the Scillies at both the Methodist and church halls, and a variety concert at the Town Hall. There was also a concert by the youth orchestra of the local school. Could deaf children appreciate music? Would it be enough for them just to watch? Jane thought it might be possible for those with a little hearing to detect the high notes of a violin, and certainly all would enjoy the percussion—they would feel the vibration. She decided to talk it over with Carole.

The following evening she tried ringing Roy Barford's Barbican number again, but there was still no answer. She'd have to ring him at the office, though she knew Roy didn't like discussing private matters on the office phone.

The next day, as it was fine, Carole suggested a trip to Pelistry Bay, a place on the east coast of St Mary's which she wanted Jane to see. It had a beach of fine golden sand, and was a treasure house of shells of all shapes and colours which would please the children. They would take their lunch with them.

Carole tried to persuade Marie to join them, but Marie had her day already mapped out. 'I'm glad to have the house to myself for a bit,' she said. 'It will give me a chance to clean my windows.'

'Not all of them?'

'No, just the rooms we use. I see one of the kids has written his name on one of the playroom windows. I hope Dr Springer didn't notice it.'

Carole laughed. 'I'm sure Luke has got far more important things on his mind than dirty windows.' Her smile slowly faded as Dinah joined them, dressed for the beach in an ankle-length cotton skirt, a stretch-nylon top that was so scanty it revealed several inches of bare midriff, and sandals that set off to perfection toenails newly varnished in red and white stripes.

Jane could sense the protest about to burst from Carole, and whispered under her breath, 'Remember what you said—"Take a little—give a little".'

Carole swallowed. 'Do you think you'll be warm enough in that dear?' she asked hollowly.

'Course I will, Mummy. Don't fuss.' Dinah looked down at herself in a doubtful way. 'You don't think it's too tight, do you? I've swelled out a bit lately.'

'I—I suppose it is a teeny-weeny bit tight—if it's uncomfortable . . .?' Carole said hopefully.

'Oh, it's comfortable enough—that's why I like it. Well, I'm ready—what about you two?'

They spent a pleasant few hours at Pelistry Bay, a secluded and delightful place with a clear view across to St Martin's and the Eastern Isles which, in the brilliant light of the Scillies, seemed very close. A causeway separated the beach from a small rocky and grassy mound called Toll's Island, which was unsafe for bathing near at high tide as the undertow was so strong. This meant keeping a watchful eye on the children as water began to creep over the causeway.

Soon after three o'clock they rounded the children up and drove back to Nightingale House. Even on that short drive some of the younger children had fallen asleep, and so had Dinah. She had caught the sun, and her midriff was bright pink. 'I warned her,' said Carole. 'I hope you've got plenty of calamine, Jane.'

Marie must have been waiting for the sound of the minibus, because as soon as Carole turned into the drive she came flying out of the front door wearing her 'agape' expression, as Luke called it. Something out of the ordinary must have happened.

'She's heard from Luke,' said Carole.

But there was the small matter of getting the children off the bus first—not something that could be hurried—before they could find out what Marie was bursting to tell them.

'It's for you, Miss—er—Jane. A phone call from America. All that way, and I heard it as plain as plain. It was your sister—she said she'd ring again at four o'clock—you've got just ten minutes. I was getting all worked up in case you didn't make it.'

Every drop of blood drained out of Jane's face. She felt limp, like a rag doll. As if from a long way away, she heard

Carole say, 'Wait for the call in Luke's study. Not the hall—you won't hear a word in the hall, not with these children stamping past. Go along, Jane, hurry!'

Jane was breathless when she reached the study. She fell into the chair by the side of the phone and stared at it, willing it to ring. Her heart was pounding so much, it drowned the ticking of the parliament clock on the wall. The minutes went slowly past. She stared around her, unseeingly at first, then slowly objects came into focus. Luke's room. A watercolour of the sun setting over Samson hung above the mantelpiece. Some boating magazines strewn about on a low table at the side of a sagging leather armchair. The roll-top desk!

The phone shrilled. Jane jumped, taken unawares at the last minute. She snatched at the receiver.

The operator said, 'I have a call from Los Angeles for you. Hold the line.'

'Jane—oh, Jane, at last!' Susan was crying—happily crying, 'Jane, darling, it's all over—the nightmare is over. The operation was successful, little Jamie is going to be all right. He came round from the anaesthetic early this morning; I'd been with him all night. I phoned Jim, and then you, but you were out—I'd forgotten the time lag. Oh, Jane, it's a miracle!'

Tears rolled down Jane's cheeks. 'How is Jamie in himself?'

'Very, very weak. He looks so frail, and his poor little head is swathed in bandages; but he smiled, Jane—he knew me. I'm sitting at his bedside now, and he's watching every move I make. I'd better hang up—I'm making such a fool of myself. I can't stop crying.'

Jane replaced the receiver feeling as if she had just come out of a long, dark tunnel into a bright new day. The sun was brighter—the colours sharper. Outside the window, a blackbird was singing—one of the loveliest sounds of spring. But there was no answering song in her heart, for she suddenly realised that her mission was over.

The plotting and scheming, the anguish and heartbreak had led to this moment. Her deception had backfired on her, but even that seemed unimportant now. Jamie had been brought back to life—that was all that mattered. She took up the receiver once more and dialled the number of the *Moonraker*.

CHAPTER ELEVEN

FAR away, in a dusty little office in a sunless court just off Fleet Street, the phone rang.

'Hello. *Moonraker*—can I help you?'

'Could you put me through to Mr Barford, please?'

'I'm sorry, he's away. Would you like to speak to someone else?'

Jane thought quickly. Who was there left on the staff she would still remember? None of the young ones stayed long enough, and she hadn't had much to do with the senior staff, except—of course, Dave McGowan. She could picture him now—the tall, thin, stooping man with a hand-rolled cigarette permanently stuck to his bottom lip. He had been chief sub-editor during her time at the *Moonraker*—a kindly man who had taken a fatherly interest in her, and helped her though many a stormy session. She asked to speak to him, and he answered in that soft Highland voice she remembered so well.

And he remembered her, too. They exchanged pleasantries. He was now deputy-editor—but not for long, he told Jane. He was retiring soon, implying by his tone that soon couldn't come quickly enough.

Roy Barford was in New York, he explained, and he didn't think he would be returning in the very near future, as he was combining business with pleasure. His primary reason for being in New York was to clinch the deal with a newspaper group who were buying up small provincial dailies and lesser-known weeklies in other countries. They had had their eye on the *Moonraker* for some time, and had made an offer Roy couldn't refuse.

'This paper needs revitalising,' said Dave frankly. 'It's been going down the drain for years. The rot set in when Roy's brother was sent to jail, the boss began to lose heart then. Then, when young Roger died, the zest went out of him completely. He did say something about going down with the flag flying—meaning one last sensational story—but nothing came of it, and last week he went off to New York. I wouldn't be surprised if he never came back to the office again.'

There was urgency in Jane's voice when she spoke again.

'Dave, can you think back to the time Roger Barford was sent to prison—four years ago, I think it was, a year after I left——'

Dave interrupted with a gentle chuckle. 'Do I remember? I should say so—we went about as if walking on eggshells. I've never seen the boss in such a mood—practically suicidal.'

'I didn't even know he had a brother,' said Jane regretfully.

'Did you not, lassie? You surprise me. But then you were always a quiet little thing—got on with your work and didn't indulge in gossip. And young Roger wasn't the kind of brother Roy would want to boast about—he'd made nothing of his life. But there, I mustn't damn the dead. It's just that we all thought young Barford was a bit of a skiver, using his dicky heart as an excuse not to exert himself, but he turned the tables on us—that's what finished him off, his heart. Well, let's get on to a happier subject. What are you doing with yourself these days, Janie? Are you still nursing, or are you married now?'

'I'm still nursing—doing a holiday job in Cornwall at the moment.' Jane began to wonder how she could politely close this conversation. Dave McGowan could be a garrulous man when he once got going.

'In Cornwall, are you? There's a coincidence for you. We had a visitor here from Cornwall yesterday, also wanting to speak to Roy Barford. Was very disappointed. He'd come all the way up from the Scilly Isles.'

Jane's heart began to pound so much, it frightened her. Her mouth went dry. 'What did he want?' she finally got out with difficulty.

'He wouldn't say—wouldn't leave his name. Big chap with black hair and shrewd blue eyes—I liked him. Not a bit like Roy Barford's usual acquaintances.'

Jane managed to say goodbye at last. She hung up, and stood leaning against the desk for support. When she felt stronger she walked to the window, staring unseeingly at the sea, seeing instead a superimposed image of Luke striding up Ludgate Hill into Fleet Street and turning into Cloverleaf Court. He had gone there to check up on her story—there was no other reason. He had gone to find out whether she had known all along about Roger Barford. He wouldn't take her word for it. Though she had felt at the time he had doubted her, she had harboured the hope that he had come to accept her explanation since. That hope now died.

The morning when he had left for Buckingham, he had been so gentle in his manner towards her, so touched by her fondness for Becky, that she had foolishly allowed herself to believe that matters would improve between them. She had deliberately put out of her mind those moments when the rift between them had seemed insurmountable, and had concentrated instead on the few—pitifully few—times when some spark of unity had seemed to ignite closer feelings. What a fool she had been! Allowing herself to be deluded into thinking she could ever mean anything to him. His world revolved around Nightingale House and little Becky, and there was no place in it for her—someone who had set out to betray him. He would never be able to forget that.

'Why is it,' she asked herself, leaning her flushed cheek against the cool glass of the window-pane, 'when everything seems to be going right with us—Fate seems to enjoy kicking us in the teeth?' A moment ago, after talking to Susan, she had felt on top of the world. Now that world was spinning around her—she felt lost.

'Jane, are you all right?' Carole stood in the doorway, her face expressive of concern. Jane straightened her shoulders and nervously smoothed her hair. She had lost all track of time.

Carole said, 'I came in to see if everything was all right, as you've been so long. Not bad news, I hope?'

Jane pulled herself together. 'No—no, it's wonderful news. The operation was successful—Jamie is going to live. He's going to be all right! I—I can't seem to take it in.' Her carefully controlled voice suddenly cracked, and she began to cry—crying happily for Jamie, crying in despair for herself.

Carole put her arms around Jane. 'Let it all come out,' she said. 'You've bottled this up too long. Luke told me a little about Jamie—not much, but I can guess what you've been through. I've walked that same path myself.'

Jane's face was blotched and red and dripping with tears, but she felt calmer. 'Sorry about that, I suppose I'm a bit hysterical. It's the relief after all those dreadful months. And for me guilt, too—I always felt responsible for Jamie's condition.'

They sat side by side on the sofa and Jane told Carole about that foggy night when the accident had happened.

'I phoned Sue late that evening to tell her Dad had had another heart attack. I wanted her with me—I felt so alone, and Sue had always been the big sister I could turn to. They came at once, Sue and Jim, all that long way from Devon, with little Jamie tucked up on the back seat. The accident happened so quickly, just after they joined the motorway, and it was a miracle Sue and Jim escaped unscathed. But poor little Jamie! And it was all so unnecessary, because Dad lingered on for a few more weeks. They could have come up the next day, in daylight, and there wouldn't have been an accident.'

'But you weren't to know that,' said Carole sensibly. 'And your father could well have died that night, and your sister would never have forgiven herself if she hadn't made the effort to come to him.'

'That's what Sue said, but I think she only said it to comfort me.'

'Why must you take all the blame on yourself, Jane? You're the most guilt-ridden person I know. Now, forget about the past—think of the future and rejoice in that. When will your sister be able to bring Jamie home?'

'We didn't get around to discussing that—Susan was crying so much, she could hardly speak. It must be catching.' Jane laughed and blew her nose. 'I can't see Jamie being allowed to be moved until the surgeon says so, and that may not be for weeks.'

'And I suppose that as soon as he is you'll be dashing off home to see him?' said Carole thoughtfully.

Jane looked down at her hands, hooding her eyes. 'My time will be up before then.'

'I'm relying on Luke to make you change your mind,' Carole said, and waited, hoping Jane would make some comment, but when she did not Carole rose to her feet, disappointed. 'Marie has put the kettle on. Would you like a cup of tea or would you prefer something stronger to celebrate with?'

Jane smiled. 'Just now I want a cup of tea more than anything. Let's leave the celebrations until later, shall we?'

Jane had a disturbing and frightening dream that night, but in a way, comforting, too. She was on Samson, but in a place like Pelistry Bay, looking out at Toll's Island. The sea was in and great waves were pounding against the rocks, and there on the islet were two small children cut off by the tide.

Jamie and Becky, clinging to each other and calling out for help in a high-pitched, reedy cry. Jane threw herself into the water to swim out to them, but the waves took hold of her and tossed her about like a piece of flotsam, and she knew she was in danger of drowning. Then Luke was beside her, his powerful arms around her, keeping her afloat. 'As long as we keep together, we'll make it,' he said. 'That's the main thing—we must keep together.'

Jane woke up. She sat up in bed, her heart racing—the dream had been so real. She could still feel Luke's arms around her, and his comforting words still rang in her ears.

But there was another sound—very plain—the steady, reedy cry for help. That was no dream—that was real. One of the children crying.

Jane switched on her bedside light, then fumbled for her slippers and dressing-gown. She hurried out of the room, down the corridor to the dormitories—the continuous, one-note cry was louder. In the room shared by six of the youngest children, the little girl they called Bubbles was sitting up in bed. She had been crying for a long time, her eyes were red and swollen. As soon as she saw Jane, she put one hand to her right ear, and shook the other hand limply—the sign for pain. She had earache.

All kinds of possibilities shot through Jane's mind—it could be something mild, or something serious like otitis media. The first thing to do was to take the child's temperature.

Jane wrapped a blanket round Bubbles and carried her to Becky's room. Better to have her here on her own, in case of infection. She slipped the thermometer into Bubbles' mouth, and when she read it was relieved to find it was normal, so the thing to do now was to treat the pain.

Warmed ear-drops were the best thing for that, and olive oil for preference. Jane wondered if there was such a thing in the house. Luke was not likely to keep any in the medicine cupboard, but there might be some in the larder. Jane thought of the larder, and her heart dropped. It was a vast cavern of a place, like an Aladdin's cave, and where would she be able to find a small bottle of olive oil in there in a hurry? She'd have to wake Marie.

Marie woke up the minute Jane tapped on her door. When Jane went in she was sitting up in bed, clutching the covers up to her neck, her hair bristling with rollers. She blinked when the light went on.

'What is it—what is it?'

Jane explained about Bubbles. 'Oh, the poor little kiddie. Yes, I've got some olive oil, I use it to make mayonnaise. I'll go down and get it for you.'

'Tell me where I can find it, I'll get it,' said Jane, but Marie wasn't having that, and they went down the stairs together. Mitzi heard them and miaowed, and Marie let her out of the cupboard, and shooed her into the garden. She found the bottle of olive oil for Jane, who warmed it in a bowl of hot water.

'Now that we're up, we may as well have a cup of tea,' said Marie, filling the kettle.

'Not for me, Marie.'

'A glass of hot milk to help you get off to sleep again, then?'

'Not even that.'

'Well, I'll just sit here and drink my tea and wait for Mitzi. I often come down of a night and let her out. She's a very clean cat—I'll say that for her!'

Bubbles had stopped whimpering. Just knowing that someone was doing something for her had dried her tears. She let Jane put the oil-drops in her ear without any fuss, and happily gulped down the orange drink in which some children's aspirin had been dissolved. Jane put a small plug of cotton wool in her bad ear and laid her on her left side. To try and explain to Bubbles in sign language that she must stay on that side to stop the oil from trickling out again was beyond her. She decided it would be easier to stay with the child until she fell asleep.

Jane drew a chair up to the window and drew back the curtains. There was a beautiful sky of palest green streaked with light at the edges where dawn was breaking. The waxing moon was very bright, and so were the few stars still shining. A peaceful night was quietly drawing to its close, and was silent except for the ceaseless murmuring of the sea.

Jane thought back to the turbulent sea of her dream, and Luke coming to save her, and both of them fighting to save the children. What had it meant? Was it a good omen?

She was frightened to see too much in it. Dreams were only one's thoughts turned into images, anyway—and her mind just lately had been dominated by thoughts of Jamie and Becky and Luke.

Luke. She gave a troubled sigh and rested her face on her hands that were gripping the window-ledge. It would be best if she never saw Luke again—if she quietly slipped away before he returned. That would save a lot of embarrassment and, for her particularly, heartbreaking emotion. For saying goodbye to him would be the hardest thing she had ever had to face.

For him, it would be no more than the termination of a contract—but, for her, leaving him and Becky—yes, and Carole and the others, too—would be like tearing up roots that went deeper than duty. She wondered about Kirsty Brownlow—often in the small hours of the night when she couldn't sleep she had thought over the story Carole had told her about Robin and Kirsty. She had thought of the 'blazing row', as Carole had called it, that Luke had had with his brother. Because Robin had wasted himself on Kirsty, Carole thought. Perhaps there was more in it than that. If Luke had had an affair with Kirsty—that solved many unanswered questions. Becky's parentage, for one thing—Luke's guilt over his brother for another.

No. She was letting her imagination run riot again. She couldn't be certain of any of this—it was all conjecture. Only one thing she did know—she didn't mean any more to Luke than someone who had filled in a necessary gap, and had done that very effectively, in spite of the ups and downs of their relationship. The thought of him thanking her, giving her a metaphorical pat on the head when it was time for her to leave, was unbearable, and it was while sitting there at that small window in Becky's room, watching the sun rise, that Jane worked out the plans for her departure.

The following day Carole took Bubbles to the hospital to have her ear examined, and came back with reassuring news. There was no infection in the ear, but there was some hard wax which could be removed by syringing it out. 'The doctor suggested you softened the wax with almond oil for a few days beforehand,' Carole told Jane. 'I brought some in with me in case Marie couldn't produce any. Marie,' she raised her voice as Marie came in from the garden with an armful of dry washing, 'would you have any almond oil in your larder?'

Marie shook her head. 'Almond oil—no. Would almond essence do?' she suggested helpfully, and wondered why the other two laughed.

Luke phoned that night. Jane was going through the hall when the phone rang, and knew instinctively who was calling. She stiffened. She hadn't the courage to answer it, she knew that once she heard Luke's deep, melodic voice again her resolution to escape would leave her. She heard Carole's quick, light footsteps in the upstairs hall, and knew she had gone to the study to take it. Jane walked on to the living-room. With the children in bed, Mitzi and her kittens had been brought out for some exercise. They were crawling over the carpet now, five black furry creatures flopping down on their fat stomachs whenever their legs gave way. Mitzi lay stretched out, her eyes half-closed, but always on the watch. Every time a kitten strayed too far away from the basket, she fetched it back, washed it and cuffed its ear. It was an occupation that was never-ending.

Carole came in bursting with information. 'That was Luke—speaking from Scott's place. He's staying there for a few days. Great news, Jane—Becky is getting on marvellously. Luke said when he visited her today she demonstrated what she'd been doing. She placed her hands either side of Luke's throat, and when he spoke she indicated that she could feel the vibration. Then she asked him to do the same to her. She made a lot of ahh-ahh-ahh sounds, and felt the vibration transmitted back to her through Luke's fingers. She's so keen, Luke said, she can hardly wait for her lessons.'

'Did Mr Arnold say she would ever speak?'

'I didn't get as far as asking that, but it's enough that she's actually making sounds and knows she is. Mr Arnold wants her for another week, then he feels Luke can carry on with the exercises. I think Luke is planning to take her back to the Arnolds later on in the summer—perhaps in August, when the two grandsons will be staying there again. In their way they're doing as much good as their grandfather. They're the first hearing children she's ever played with, and somehow she seems to understand them. She has to, Luke said—as they won't make any allowances for her.'

Jane was thinking, one more week—I've got one more week to work everything out in detail.

As soon as she knew the day of Luke's expected return she would book her passage on the helicopter. She wanted to time her departure to coincide with Luke's arrival, so that afterwards nobody could accuse her of walking out on the children. It was only her guilty conscience that prompted such thoughts—the children were in no danger with Carole and Marie around, but they had been left in her charge, so she must stay with them until the last possible moment.

June so far had lived up to its name; now it turned cold and wet, and picnics on the beach were out of the question. For the next few days, the children, well wrapped up in waterproofs, were herded into places of interest and well doctrinated into the social life of the Scillies, both past and present. They loved it—everything was of interest to them because Carole and Jane made it interesting, and also because they usually finished up in a café, often overlooking the sea, where they could stuff themselves with chocolate fudge cake washed down with glasses of fruit squash.

On one occasion, when they got home with rainwater running off their coats and leaking into their boots, they were met by Marie with the news that Luke had just phoned to say he would be arriving on Friday, just after midday, coming on the *Scillonian*. Today was Wednesday—Jane knew she had to think fast.

That afternoon she phoned the airport, and booked a seat on the ten-past-one flight on the tenth. As she replaced the receiver she thought, That's it—finished. She felt drained.

Friday, as if to welcome the travellers home, dawned clear and bright with not a cloud to be seen. 'I know,' said Carole. 'We'll take the children to Porthcressa. We can laze in deck-chairs while they play on the sands, and then we can all walk to the quay to see the *Scillonian* come in.'

'I wonder why Luke is making the crossing by sea rather than flying?' queried Dinah.

'Perhaps he couldn't get seats. The helicopters are usually fully booked this time of year.'

Jane felt that Fate had taken a hand in her affairs, for she had no difficulty in getting a seat. Now she had to find a plausible excuse for not going with the others, but even that proved no difficulty, for Carole approached her rather diffidently and asked would she do her a favour? 'Marie will insist on cooking a big roast for our midday meal—says it's to welcome Luke and Becky home. She wants us all to sit together, even the children, in the dining-room. She can't do all the preparations herself. Would you mind staying behind and helping her, Jane?'

Yes, thought Jane, Fate is decidedly taking a hand in my affairs. And she wasn't all that happy about it.

But she did enjoy laying out the big dining-room table, extending it to its fullest length and adding another smaller table to it. There was no tablecloth big enough to cover both, so she used a sheet, then two lace-edged cloths, cornerwise to cover that. She laid up with the best silver and china and cut glass and, as a finishing touch, put a silver candelabrum in the centre of the table with a ring of pansies at its base. When Marie saw the end result her thin face glowed with pleasure.

'You've made it look a real treat,' she said. 'Just like Christmas—which reminds me. I've got some red paper serviettes somewhere, I'll fish them out—they'll give a nice finishing touch. You've got a way with you, Miss—er—er—Jane. I couldn't have made it look so nice.'

'Is there anything else I could do for you—the vegetables?'

'I got up early and did those before breakfast. The meat's doing nicely—all I've got to do now is beat up the Yorkshire pudding and make the white sauce for the broad beans. When you're ready I'll make us some coffee.'

Jane had already tidied her bedrom, stripped the bed and folded up the used sheets and pillowcases ready for the wash. Her case she had packed the night before, but left open for last-minute things. She changed now into her jeans and shaggy jumper—then she went along to Luke's room to ring for a taxi, and to leave a note she had written to him the night before.

She had agonised over what to say. The first draft had been so unfeeling, so matter-of-fact, not what she wanted to say at all, and she had torn it up. Her final attempt was a *cri de coeur*—and why not? She wasn't ashamed of her love—so long as she was some distance away when Luke learnt about it. She had written,

Dear Luke,

Please forgive me for running off like this. I'm doing so because I can't face you—not feeling the way I do about you. I know I don't mean anything to you—except that sometimes you find me useful, and other times, I think I can safely say, good company. But mostly you get impatient with me, and you'll never, never get over your distrust of me.

I found out about you trying to see Roy Barford to check up on me, and that hurt dreadfully. If I didn't love you I would have been angry, not hurt—as it is, it made me realise that there is no hope for a better relationship between us.

That's why I'm going away now, before you return. If I stayed I might break down and make a total fool of myself, and I want to spare you the embarrassment of that. I only feel safe when I'm away from you—by the time you read this I shall be on my way to Penzance.

There's a lot more I would like to say to you, but there's really no point as we won't meet again. Please try not to think too badly of me.

God bless you,
Jane

She took her case downstairs and left it in the

hall. The postman had called in the meantime, and Marie had put the letters on the hall-table. Among them were two airmail letters—one addressed to herself from Susan, and the other for Luke, postmarked Vancouver. A letter from the mysterious Kirsty Brownlow? But that no longer mattered. Jane put Susan's letter in her bag to read later, then walked resolutely towards the kitchen.

Marie was sitting at the table, grating cheese for the sauce. Her eyes widened when she saw Jane, for she could tell by her attitude that something was wrong. There was a look of desperation in Jane's dark eyes, but at the same time a determined tilt to her chin. Slowly Marie looked Jane up and down, taking in her travelling outfit of jeans and shaggy jumper, the shoulder bag and anorak she was carrying. She rose to her feet.

'You're leaving,' she said accusingly.

Jane nodded. 'I've come to say goodbye, Marie. Would you please tell Carole I shall be writing to her, and I've left a note of explanation for Dr Springer on his desk.'

Marie gave a sharp intake of breath. 'You mean you're sneaking off without them knowing?'

'I'm going a few days earlier, that's all. It's just to save a lot of embarrassment—and tears, too. I just can't face saying goodbye.'

Marie leant heavily on the table, putting her weight on her hands. 'Did you know Mrs Springer was arranging a farewell party for you? It was to be a surprise. We've been baking things between us, hiding them from you. This setting up the dining-room table today was just a rehearsal. That's how it was going to be for the party—and now you're running out on us——' Words failed Marie; she took out her handkerchief and blew her nose. Jane's eyes watered.

'Please, Marie, don't make it any harder for me. I don't want to run away like this. To be truthful, I don't want to leave Nightingale House at all, but I've got to, and it's

best for everyone's sake that I go quietly and without any
fuss.'

'What about Becky? What will she think when she finds
you gone . . .?' Marie's protests faded. The anguish she saw
in Jane's face stopped her. 'How are you going to get to the
airport?' she asked woodenly.

'By taxi—it's due any minute now.'

'You've got it all worked out nicely, haven't you?' Marie
was bitter, then she relented and came round the table to
Jane, and wrapped her in her bony arms. 'I don't like saying
goodbye, either, so you won't mind if I don't come and see
you out. Just take care of yourself, that's all. Go along—I
can hear the taxi.'

On the way to the airport, Jane read Susan's letter. Dr
Tollesbury was so pleased with the outcome of the
operation that he had said if Jamie continued to make such
good progress he could leave the clinic in two weeks' time,
on the understanding that he would have to be nursed
carefully for several months to come. Susan finished, 'He
has suggested that Jamie has a course of physiotherapy to
help get back the use of his limbs. That's something we can
arrange between us, Jane, when I'm home again.'

Jane replaced the letter in its envelope and stared with a
faraway look out of the taxi window. Dear Jamie, if she
could only keep her mind on him—think of him running
and playing and laughing again—perhaps she could forget
the pain of her own despair.

She was due to collect her ticket fifteen minutes before
the flight left for Penzance, but she had more than half an
hour to spare when she arrived at the airport. She fetched a
cup of coffee from the counter and sat in the window
overlooking the flightpath. St Mary's airport was bigger
than the heliport at Penzance, because it not only served the
helicopters, but also the fixed winged planes from airports

in southern England and the Skybus service from Land's End.

She watched as one of these small aircraft now touched down on the runway. About ten people, a full complement of passengers, alighted from the Skybus, among them a tall, broad-shouldered man and a small black-haired girl.

Jane's blood froze in her veins, and for a moment she felt lifeless. Then she jumped to her feet in such haste that she sent her cup of coffee flying. She had to hide—any minute now Luke would come through that door. She looked about her in a wild fashion. There was only one place to hide—the Ladies'.

Ten minutes later, she emerged, looking carefully about her. The lounge was filling up with the next lot of homebound travellers. One of the girls from behind the counter was mopping up the spilt coffee, and she gave Jane a reproachful look.

'I'm sorry,' said Jane lamely. 'I was in a hurry. I suppose you wouldn't have noticed a tall man and a little girl, both with black hair?'

'You've missed them. They caught a taxi.'

With a sinking feeling of relief, Jane went to the reception counter to collect her ticket. 'I'm afraid I haven't got you booked in on the next flight,' the official told her.

'But I phoned on Wednesday. I booked a seat on the ten-past-one helicopter.'

The official looked through the lists for every flight that day. 'I'm sorry, miss—but there must have been a mistake.'

'But there can't have been. I was told quite clearly. The ten-past-one on the tenth.'

'It's not the tenth today, it's the ninth,' the man answered patiently, pointing to the almanac on the counter.

Jane went cold. Of course it was the ninth. How had she come to make such a stupid mistake? 'Is there a spare seat on any other flight?'

'I'm sorry, miss—fully booked, and all flights tomorrow, too, except for the seat already reserved for you.' His manner was sympathetic. 'If you need to get to Penzance today, there's the *Scillonian*.' But the *Scillonian* didn't leave until five-fifteen—she had to get away before then. The man was saying, 'If you want to cancel your booking, would you please fill in this form?'

'Could I leave it for now? I'll be back.' Jane suddenly felt in awful danger. She wasn't safe at the airfield—it was only a short distance by car from Nightingale House, and she had already wasted precious minutes—and there was the possibility that Luke might come after her.

She ran out of the building, leaving her case and anorak behind. They could be dealt with later, too; they'd be quite safe. She looked about her, hoping to see a spare taxi, but was unlucky. She could have phoned for one, but she wanted to be on the move—she felt very vulnerable, waiting here on this flat, open stretch of land. She followed the concrete track that linked the airfield to the road, a quarter-of-a-mile walk which she covered in a few minutes. There was a bus-stop on the corner—dared she take a chance that a bus might happen along? The bus would take her to Old Town, where she could lie low, even find bed-and-breakfast accommodation, and, tomorrow being Saturday, the *Scillonian* made two sailings. She could leave on the first at nine-forty-five tomorrow morning.

She was standing there, biting her knuckles, when she caught the sound of the Triumph Spitfire, and a moment later the little red car came hurtling round the bend—straining to the last of its horsepower. In a panic, Jane sprinted across the road—there was a footpath there that led to a nature trail through a pine wood. It meant cover—and all Jane could think about then was cover!

After the heavy rain of the past few days, the track through the trees was one long chain of puddles. Jane slithered in the mud, splashing her jeans up to her knees, and running blindly—and for no purpose. She could hear a crashing on broken branches and twigs in the undergrowth—Luke was following, and rapidly gaining on her.

He caught up with her just where the trees spread out to make a small clearing. Cornered, she turned on him, and began to lash out at him with her fists. He roared with laughter and swung her up in his arms. 'Have I got to carry you all the way back to the car, or will you walk sensibly like a good girl?' he said.

'You needn't speak to me in that fashion—I'm not a child!'

'Then stop behaving like one! Running away from me—hitting out at me! What good did you think that would do?' He stared down at her, saw the distress in her eyes and the anxious twitching of her mouth, and the creases of laughter in his face faded. He stood her gently on her feet, and tilted back her head so that he could kiss her—a very tender and lingering kiss. 'That's only an example,' he said. 'They'll improve. I've had three weeks to think about them—I'm saving the best for last.'

He's laughing at me, thought Jane. He's playing with me. In a stupor, she let him walk her to the car, making no effort to break away from his hold. Every now and then, unable to check his laughter, he would come out with a sudden guffaw. Each time he did so, Jane shrivelled a little bit more.

'Where's your case?' he asked as he closed the car door on her.

'At the airport.'

'It can wait.' He turned the car and headed back the way he had come. He passed the end of the lane that led to Nightingale House, and drove on to the bay where the old butty was beached. Across the water, Samson shimmered in the sunlight.

'Remember this place?' he asked.

'Yes. It's from here we sailed across to Samson, my first Sunday——'

'The day it happened,' he said softly. 'The day I fell in love with you.'

She twisted her hands in anguish. 'You're playing with me.'

'I'm deadly serious.' He pulled her round to face him. The sunlight intensified the blue of his eyes. The strain and worry that had marred his features for days were gone; he looked like a man at peace. His arms went round her, and he was kissing her as if he had a hunger for her that could never be appeased. 'I told you it would get better,' he whispered against her mouth.

'I thought you were laughing at me.'

'I was laughing because I was happy. I was laughing at the way you turned on me—like a little hell-cat. There are hidden passions in you, my love, that I never guessed at.'

Jane settle against his shoulder, surrendering herself to the aura of happiness that blocked out the doubts and misgivings and suspicions of the past.

Luke said, 'It would be fine to just sit here, enjoying being together—but there are things we must get straightened out first.'

Tenderly, he drew his hand across her hair and down the line of her cheek. She caught it in her own, and held it to her lips and kissed it, then snuggled back in his arms to listen to the music of his voice as he made so many things plain to her.

'First of all your letter—oh, Jane, that letter! Marie told me it was waiting for me. I came down those stairs like a bat out of hell to get to the car—to get to you. I knew I had a good chance of catching you if I put a move on. Yes, I had been to see Roy Barford—not to check up on you, as you thought, but to ask him about Jamie's fees at the Tollesbury Clinic. I wanted to pay them; I also wanted to repay any expenses Barford had already incurred.' He stifled Jane's protests. 'Listen, darling—I can afford it. Robin left money in trust for children, mainly for deaf children—but for any child in need.'

He went on, 'Roy Barford thought there was some powerful reason for me giving up my Home Office work and going off to Tuscany, and he was right—there was. Not scandal, as he hoped—I had health problems.' Jane jerked upright, but he pulled her back. 'Everything is all right now, that's what I want to tell you.

'You already know that my brother Ned died of an acute form of aplastic anaemia—a disease that destroys the red and white cells and the platelets in the bone marrow. I didn't know that Robin was suffering from a chronic form of the same disease until he wrote and told me about a year later. I'd been feeling out of sorts myself for some time—excessive tiredness and breathlessness on exertion. I wondered if I were a third victim. I went to a colleague, a physician who specialises in blood disorders, but he could neither confirm nor rebut my diagnosis. He advised me to take a course of treatment which included regular blood transfusions, and I carried on with this for months—until I thought, to hell with it all. I'll chuck up work and go and see Robin. I wanted to make my peace with him—we'd had a bitter row some time previously.

'As soon as I saw Robin I knew he hadn't got long to live. I couldn't leave him then. And he had this pretty little toddler living with him, little Becky—his daughter.'

'I thought she was your daughter,' Jane said in a small voice.

'I guessed you did—and Carole suspected Becky was Ned's.' Luke sounded remorseful. 'Looking back now, I realise I shouldn't have been so secretive, but I did it for a good reason—at least, I thought so at the time.'

He turned to Jane and tilted her face to his. 'I've made a lot of stupid blunders in my time, but the worst blunder of all was ever to doubt you for one moment. My only excuse is that I've been under a lot of pressure—health problems, etcetera—I couldn't think straight at times. The nightmare of uncertainty is over now, thank God.'

He told Jane about the stormy relationship that had existed between Kirsty and Robin, of their parting, and the daughter Robin knew nothing about, born prematurely in Mexico where Kirsty was then touring, and farmed out to local peasants.

'She didn't want Robin's child,' said Luke flatly. 'I learnt later that she tried to have an abortion. Once the baby was born she got rid of it quickly enough, thinking that, by paying generously for the child's care, she had discharged her duty. A friend wrote and told Robin about the little girl living in a remote part of Mexico, who was possibly his daughter. Robin immediately got in touch with Kirsty and, after much haggling, she gave permission for him to become Becky's guardian. He was shattered when he discovered that Becky was deaf, and blamed himself for not finding out about her sooner. She had been cared for by simple, loving folk, but they had accepted her handicap as inevitable and had done nothing about it.

'Even then, Robin wouldn't allow any criticism of Kirsty. He still loved her deeply and, because he wanted to protect her from adverse publicity, he didn't want anybody to know she was Becky's mother. He was so frightened the media would get hold of the story—and what that might do to Kirsty's reputation. As sick as he was, all he could think about was protecting her.'

Silence fell between them. Jane, stealing a look at Luke, saw the distress signals in his face—the telling of that unhappy episode had stirred up unwanted memories.

'Robin made me his executor,' he said after a pause. 'He left a considerable fortune, requesting me to use it for the benefit of children like Becky—that's how I came to think of a place like Nightingale House——' He broke off, sidetracked by something else. 'There are many holiday homes for deaf children run by official societies. I couldn't hope to compete with those—I just wanted a small, friendly little place where Becky could mix with her own kind.' He returned to his former subject. 'I stayed on in Tuscany for a few years after Robin died, getting to know Becky better—winding up Robin's affairs. I took my time. I was in no hurry to get back to London—Italy agreed with me, and my health improved. During that time I repeatedly tried to persuade Kirsty to allow me to adopt Becky, but she refused out of sheer cussedness. She hated me, and wouldn't do anything that might afford me pleasure.'

Luke took the airmail letter that had come that morning out of his pocket. 'This changes everything,' he said. 'At last Kirsty agrees to my terms. I think it was the large sum of money I used as bait that decided her. Obviously her career isn't so successful as it was.' He gave a sigh of pleasure. 'So now I can openly proclaim to the world that Becky is my daughter.' He chuckled. 'Poor Carole, I should have been honest with her. But I was trying to be loyal to Robin, still protecting Kirsty's name, and also I didn't want to say anything while Becky's future still hung in the balance. That's all over with now, and I'll make my peace with Carole when I see her.'

'Do you think she's still waiting on the quay for you? She thought you were coming over on the *Scillonian*.' Jane reminded him.

Luke thought that funny. Sad memories had gone, he looked free from care, his blue eyes gleaming with laughter. 'I did, too. But I had a blow-out on the motorway—that delayed me, and I missed the boat. Just by lucky chance

I got the last two seats on the Skybus—and arrived earlier than if I'd come on the ferry.'

'And frightened the life out of me!'

He gave her a tender smile, and a more than tender kiss. 'Never be frightened of me, Jane. Never think you have anything to fear. I laughed at the way you ran from me—but I was hurt, too——'

She put her hand over his mouth. 'Let's not think back, let's think only of the present.'

'And the future, Jane. Our future, and Becky's future—a ready-made family. That's what I dreamed of, but all the time the doubt about my health clouded everything   en my judgement of you.'

'When you were staying with Scott, did you take the opportunity of seeing your physician again?'

'Scott made me. He said I was a fool to have put if off for so long. I told the physican that if he gave me a clean bill of health I'd go straight back home and ask a certain beautiful girl to marry me—and he obliged! He told me that tests showed that I'm cured of whatever it was that was destroying my blood cells, and said there was good hope that the bone marrow may gradually regain its haemopoietic function. I came out of his surgery walking on air, with only one thought in my mind—to get back to you as quickly as possible. I thought of all the times I'd been cruel to you, snide in my remarks——'

'That's coming it a bit strong,' said Jane fondly.

He laughed. 'And you feel no resentment?' He cupped her face in his hands and looked deep into her genle, loving eyes. 'When a man is eaten up by love and can't express it, he acts like a fool—that's my only excuse.'

She buried her hands in his hair, pulled his face down to the level of hers and stopped his mouth with her lips. Luke took a deep breath. 'If you do that too often,' he said, 'I shan't be responsible for my actions.'

She lent across him and switched on the ignition. 'I think it's time we went back and made our peace with the others, and——'

As if unsatisfied, Luke drew her close to him again.

'Think of that succulent roast in the oven,' Jane said.

Luke switched off the ignition again. 'Dinner can wait,' he said. 'This can't!'

Unwrap romance this Christmas

A Love Affair
LINDSAY ARMSTRONG

Valentine's Night
PENNY JORDAN

Man on the Make
ROBERTA LEIGH

Rendezvous in Rio
ELIZABETH OLDFIELD

Put some more romance into your Christmas, with four brand new titles from Mills & Boon in this stylish gift pack.

They make great holiday reading, and for only £5.40 it makes an ideal gift.

The special gift pack is available from 6th October. Look out for it at Boots, Martins, John Menzies, W.H. Smith, Woolworths and other paperback stockists.